# HUMANITY'S

# ENDGAME

## Eve Langlais

NEW YORK TIMES & USA TODAY BESTSELLING AUTHOR

## PROLOGUE

The stench of despair and death surrounded me. I'd finally run out of luck. In this dark and dirty place, I'd finally entered the last stage of my life.

The endgame.

How had it come to this?

Five years ago, I thought the most pressing thing I had to worry about was how many people liked my latest selfie. The moment I'd post my very contrived picture—selected from about fifty—I was checking to see who liked it. Did anyone comment? Who could I see active online not responding at all?

Back then I worried about all the wrong things. Petty things that took up my entire day when I wasn't at work. And by work I meant the mindless drone of answering phones and making appointments for people in need of dental work.

Facing certain, painful death, I missed my old life. Wished I'd not wasted those days when everything was going so fucking good. I could eat whenever I wanted, whatever I desired. Slept in a warm, clean, and comfortable bed. Knew nine-one-one was a phone call away if I needed help.

Then it happened. The world ended.

Not because of climate change—and for the curious, the only thing that improved after humanity stopped polluting was the smog. The weather remained just as unpredictable.

Because of the predicted nuclear apocalypse? Wrong, although it did come close when North Korea had a missile malfunction. That was the end of that dictatorship.

So what destroyed humanity?

Remember the COVID pandemic of 2020? Nope, it wasn't that.

Nothing compared to the virus that wiped out billions of people. We had no cure. No way of stopping it. After all, it wasn't manmade or from an animal on earth.

Aliens did it.

I still remember snorting in disbelief as the president of the United States, a man abhorred by half the nation, adored by the other, gave a speech, live streamed to everyone in the world and said, "My fellow Americans, we've made contact."

## CHAPTER 1

Lips pursed for the ultimate selfie—the pose called duck lips, a pouting thing that made me look sultrier—I found myself distracted when the waiting room for the dental group I worked for erupted into noisy chatter.

Apparently, the president was giving an impromptu speech.

Boring. Like I cared what some old dude had to say. One president or another, they were all the same. Constantly arguing. Claiming the last guy sucked. Making promises that were never kept.

Blah. Blah. Blah.

But then I heard a word that peaked my interest.

Aliens.

Say what?

It didn't take long to find the live stream. I played it from the beginning.

"Citizens of the United States of America, what I am about to tell you is shocking, perhaps even scary, but I want to assure you that you have nothing to fear."

Wrong thing to say. My stomach immediately fluttered.

Had Russia finally declared war? The media had been saying we needed to watch them for years, or was it China? Depending on the people in power, the enemy changed. Could even be that man in North Korea who liked wear his hair in a bowl cut.

I'd lost track of who was more of a threat to the USA. Personally, I thought we should watch those sneaky Canadians. Always apologizing, hoarding their maple syrup, eating beaver's tails. Shudder.

The president then said the most unexpected thing. "My fellow Americans, we've made contact."

Well, that shut everyone in the press gallery right the fuck up. Except for one smartass, who said, "Bullshit."

"I assure you, it's quite true, and you don't have to take my word for it. We have proof."

Ha, as if. I still remembered that supposed space truck or something the government claimed to have in their possession a while back. Internet rumors claimed it was just some futuristic imagined car. Given it was the year of the COVID pandemic, no one paid it much mind.

The screen to the president's left began showing all kinds of boring stuff. Science mumbo jumbo about how they'd been sending signals into space. Watching for unusual movements and patterns. I fast forwarded until I was live with the briefing, which was when they finally got to the good part.

Apparently, those science geeks sending out 'Hello, anyone out there?' signals got a reply back.

There was skepticism. "How do you know you're not being pranked?" An understandable concern, given the spacecar thing had spawned all kind of theories.

A scientist took over at this point and went into more incomprehensible jargon about how they'd authenticated the message. How the hell did one verify a message really came from aliens? Was I the only one who wondered if he'd been punked?

It was inevitable that this declaration of having made contact brought mention of Space Force. "Mr.

President, what will Space Force do to ensure this supposed contact doesn't threaten our country?"

"I'm glad you asked. The good news is we've been preparing for a while now because we knew we weren't alone out here in this great universe. But the better news is, all those defense mechanisms we've installed won't be necessary. The aliens come in peace."

Of course, someone just had to say, "Isn't the term alien derogatory?"

"For the moment, we don't have a better term, but I'm sure once we've established diplomatic relations, we'll be able to come up with a name they consider suitable."

Ooh, well played.

"Are they already here?" a reporter shouted from the back, the usual decorum being tossed out the window.

The president answered. "No. But we are expecting our first delegation shortly."

The press corps erupted, shouting questions, most of which had no answers.

At that point, I tuned out and my mind went inward.

Aliens were real. Would they be human-killing monsters like in the movies?

Would they infect us so that alien babies burst from our bellies?

Take us as slaves?

Most important of all, I wondered if they were cute.

## CHAPTER 2

THE PRESENT

MY STOMACH GRUMBLED. MY OWN FAULT. I'D waited until I got down to my last can of corn, only to discover it had gone rancid when I opened it.

I almost cried. But I didn't want to waste the fluids. The rancid can of corn got tossed in my compost heap in the apartment next door. I'd been trying to grow stuff but wasn't having much luck despite placing it in front of a window that got sunlight. The best I'd managed was a few tiny carrots.

Delicious I might add.

Inside my own place, darkness reigned, the windows covered over so that, at night, no light could peek out. I'd checked and double-checked that I remained hidden. Just like every day, I made sure my traps were set, the ones that would warn me if someone, or something, came inside. A string of cans strung in the hall. Garbage in front of the stairwell door that would clatter if toppled.

Thus far, I'd been lucky. I'd been living here for about five months. One hundred and forty seven days by the marks I'd made on my wall.

Actually, Karen's wall. I'd taken over her apartment and, with nothing better to do, had dug into her life. Karen enjoyed puzzles, knitting, and sweaters. So many sweaters.

I didn't wear one for my upcoming foraging trip. I preferred form-fitting, and dark, the better to blend with shadows as I did my best to slip around unseen.

Once upon a time, I wanted to be seen. Now...I dreaded it.

I waited until well after dawn before venturing outside. There was a time I used to avoid the sunlight. When the virus first hit, it didn't take long to realize the symptoms of it got worse in the daytime, which ran contrary to every horror movie I'd ever watched.

Something about the UV rays interacting with the alien spores released on Earth made the air dangerous to breathe, hence why I wore a mask the moment I stepped out of my safe room, which was on the second floor of a multi-unit building. Now, you might ask, why not the penthouse?

I will mention, in the early days of the world's end, when people died in the streets, some by the virus, others because madness reigned, I thought to myself, if I'm going to die, I want to do so in luxury. I walked—and ran—to a condo I'd always admired and rode the elevator up to the top floor, where I encountered a locked door that required an axe. Which it should be noted is not as easy to swing as you'd imagine. Noisy too. But once I managed to whack my way through, I claimed the most luxurious space for myself.

A few weeks later, with no one to monitor the electrical grid, the power went out. It never returned and twenty-five flights of stairs was nobody's idea of fun. My huffing-and-puffing ass relocated. Several places as it turned out over the next five years. I discovered it was easier to find a new building with many units I could scavenge as my base than forage and lug back stuff.

This time, I'd exhausted not only the apartment complex I'd chosen but the entire block it perched on. It was time to go looking for a new home.

As I crept outside, I remained alert. Only dead people didn't pay attention to their environment, just like only the stupid didn't hide at the first noise or hint of movement.

I remember my first attack vividly. It was a wonder I didn't die that first week after civilization ended. But I learned from my mistakes. Even had the scars to prove it.

My soft-soled shoes didn't make a sound as I tread carefully forth. I hated the idea of leaving my safe room; however, I'd stripped this building of usable food and items.

Hunger tightened my belly and demanded I be brave and go forth and find a place where dry staples and canned goods gathered dust in empty apartments.

At least being in the city, I had plenty to scavenge, but I remained conscious I wasn't alone. Although I saw signs of other people less and less as time passed.

In the beginning of the apocalypse, I used to run into folks, some of them the good kind that I hung with for a bit. Yet, after a while, either they got careless and killed or they moved on.

Me? I was too scared to leave the city and the surety of finding food hidden in dusty cupboards. For much too long, I also held on to the hope that help would come. I didn't want to be lost in the wilderness when it did.

That hope eventually faded. As did my encounters with people. These days, loneliness threatened me most. What I wouldn't give to hear another human voice. To feel someone's touch. Masturbating was all well and good, but I missed someone going down on me.

A hug would be nice as well.

Hell, at this point, I'd suck a dick even if I never got the appeal before.

The street outside the building had weeds growing up through the pavement. Each spring, after the winter melt, nature took back more and more of the city. Neatly pruned trees grew wild. Windows cracked over time, and the glass shards littered the pavement. The one thing not seen that I'd expected from the movies was the scraps of paper being tossed around, maybe even a tumbleweed for shits and giggles.

The reality proved more stark.

And inescapable.

The city was a dead place. I knew it, and yet, I couldn't seem to bring myself to muster the courage to leave. Although, every time I changed buildings, I moved closer to the edge of the city. On foot.

See, I didn't own a car when the virus hit. Like many, I locked myself away, and hoped I wouldn't get sick and die. I'd seen the videos before the internet shut down.

People sweating and crying out, their bodies thrashing. Dying in agony. But that seemed preferable to what happened to the others.

By the time it occurred to me I should leave town, the transit system had shut down. I didn't have a car. I couldn't rent one, or even pay for a ride.

The services I relied on quit, leaving me with only my two feet. It was why I'd gone only about five miles in five years. That and fear.

Every time I left my hidey-hole I exposed myself. What if someone—something...—spotted me? Attacked me in the open or followed me home?

What if I wasn't careful enough when it came to protecting myself and I got sick? For all that being alone sucked, I didn't want to die.

But my biggest fear of all was what if I got to the edge of the city and there was nothing? Just even more quiet streets and dead houses. Less food because suburbia tended to be more spread out. Although maybe I could grow some vegetables.

And kill them with my epically bad, gardening instincts.

My foreboding wasn't helped by the fact I'd not seen any animals in a long time. Not normal ones at any rate. I didn't like to think of that thing I'd once seen that might have been a cat. Leaping down from a lamppost, its body wider than normal and tiny legs growing from it. Its eyes a milky white.

Nightmares now walked the Earth. Had everything died or become perverted?

My foot scuffed pavement, and in my mind, I might as well have blown a bugle shouting, *"Here I am!"*

I paused. Sweated a bit. Put my hand on the comforting weight of the gun by my side. A false confidence since I'd not practiced using it. Didn't even know if it would fire. Which was why I also had a knife in a sheath, plus another strapped to my calf.

You couldn't hesitate or give into squeamishness in the apocalypse.

Nothing moved, and yet I breathed hard inside my mask, making myself lightheaded. I wanted to rip it off and gulp the air, but I kept my mask on. I'd not remained alive this long to be stupid now.

At times, though, I wondered if I should bother. I remembered all the arguments on masks. None truly fully filtered virus particles. So explain how I remained alive? What if removing it finally allowed the virus to take root.

The mask stayed on.

And as I continued on my quest for a new apartment, I remembered the day the world technically ended.

## CHAPTER 3
THE PAST

THE WORLD BUZZED WITH EXCITEMENT.

Two days after the president's announcement that they'd made contact with aliens, everyone talked about what first contact would mean.

Some saw it as a positive thing, others as a calamity. You could class the opinions into a few groups.

The jealous country leaders who lost out to that brash American when it came to first contact. For once, the American media united and thumbed their respective noses and took pride in the fact aliens recognized the USA's greatness.

The next kind of people were the ones who claimed they knew aliens existed all along and it would bring a new age of enlightenment. The sale of

*Star Trek* uniforms and even *Stars War* ensembles rocketed.

Then there were the doomsayers. The end was nigh. The religious repented. They also bought guns. Food. Everything they could get their hands on.

Me?

I went shopping for a new outfit. I wasn't alone. Many of my generation were giddy about meeting alien life.

And finally, there was one final group, who, as usual, contradicted everything the president said. But not many people listened to their rabid ranting about the head of the republic. They despised him, so they weren't about to take his word. Nor did they accept his proof or the testimony of scientists. The opposition party claimed the president mentally unfit and in need of removal. Screamed it loud and for everyone to hear.

In response, the president released more footage and even more alien artifacts, hidden until now.

It didn't help.

Heads exploded. Suddenly he was betraying the country by giving away their secrets.

*Remove him from office!* Having heard the word impeach so many times—every time a president was elected at this point—the populace had become immune to it. Which didn't improve the situation because, as everyone lost their collective minds—again, as they seemed to do every other day now—the aliens entered our galaxy, and everyone with a powerful telescope could see it. It became the point where no one could deny something was coming.

What, though? No one quite knew. Messages didn't translate into images. Or so the government claimed. All we had to go on? A smudge moving through space.

Could be a meteor, only it appeared guided, rapid in its trajectory, and avoiding things in its path.

Telescopes sent a constant stream of images showing a sphere. Massive, kind of Deathstar-ish in appearance. I will admit, I dug out my Princess Leia costume and wasn't the only one at the Halloween party wearing braided coils at the club. The guy who got into my panties was no Han Solo, but he made me see stars.

The giant sphere came alone, and we began communicating more rapidly, apparently with the aliens. Not by voice though. The aliens replied in English to all queries.

They said it was easier for them to learn than to teach us their language. I wasn't the only one who burned at the perceived insult.

The fearful doubled in number overnight and demanded our government stop the alien invasion.

*"We're paying for Space Force. Why aren't we deploying it?"* had screamed a lifelong politician. A few years ago, they'd been among those mocking its creation.

The president held firm. "They come in peace."

Oddly enough, his words brought forth a new movement, those who created signs that said Welcome. I hung out with them for a few nights. Their weed was good. The sex? Mediocre given guys who are high aren't that motivated.

The funniest thing during that time? The sale on butt plugs skyrocketed according to reports. The term #saynotoanalprobes began trending.

I bought clean underwear and lube. I still had hope the aliens would be cute and single. Speculation abounded, but no one knew for sure what to expect. It led to Borg memes making the rounds.

As the arrival date approached, the streets got chaotic. As with all things in this decade, when people got upset, riots erupted. My boss gave me the week off, but unlike many on my street, I wasn't clearing shelves in supermarkets and hoarding. I practiced my potential speech in the mirror.

"Hello there, handsome. How was the trip?" Too husky? Maybe I needed to go a bit higher.

I smiled. More like a grimace in the mirror.

What if the aliens were intelligent, but ugly? I liked to think I wasn't that shallow.

I channeled an old sitcom and winked. "How you doing?"

What if there was a language barrier? What if smiling with teeth was an insult? Or eye contact? Could be that aliens didn't flirt the same way as humans.

All those thoughts ran through my head, never mind my chance of meeting alien life was like zero. Dental secretaries in their twenties didn't have access to top secret meetings with extraterrestrial life, but hey, a girl could dream.

The day arrived.

Like the rest of the world—who wasn't drinking the poison juice as some preached the end of the world—I was glued to my computer where a website streamed the arrival live.

Oh, the crying by the networks when a certain billionaire bought the rights to the broadcast, and then dared to show it for free. Uncut. No commercials.

I don't think I blinked as the camera panned to

catch the appearance of the big globe in the sky. It hovered before sinking gracefully. Not a crashing meteor as some predicted.

It landed and appeared smoother than expected, the outer shell gray in color, having little texture.

When the sphere hit the water, it didn't even cause a splash.

*Oooh.* I swear I heard the world exhale.

A gangplank, narrow and without support, extended from the ship to the dock where the president and his entourage stood.

The door to the vessel opened.

I held my breath. Aliens. Holy fuck. I couldn't believe this was happening.

Little did I know, it was the beginning of the end.

## CHAPTER 4
THE PRESENT

THE NEXT BLOCK OVER, CHAFING BEHIND THE mask I used to protect me, I saw a potential building, about six stories, the balconies out front an indication they were apartments. The vestibule had been trashed, but a long time ago judging by the layer of filth on everything.

Not by monsters. In the end, it wasn't the aliens that attacked humanity but the survivors of the plague.

Those changed by the experience attacked the rest. Guess I couldn't mock those movies or television shows anymore. I'd always scoffed at the idea we'd turn on each other in the final hour. But here we were, playing humanity's endgame, the moment we should have worked together for the greater good.

Instead, we reverted to some primal version where survival trumped empathy.

For a second, I debated not even bothering checking the upper floors; however, I knew for a fact sometimes those squatting were lazy and would avoid any effort, such as climbing stairs.

A hand on my gun, sweating hard and stinking. It wouldn't be noise that would give me away but the stench of me. When you lived alone, things like deodorant every day lost all meaning.

I'd need to bathe after this. Coiled, I tensed as I went up each step, especially as I turned each corner on the landing between floors. As I moved upward, I noticed the doors leading to the first and second floor were heavily damaged. No point checking apartments. I found a body on the landing of the third. Decayed and chewed to the point the skull grinned at me.

But it was the extra parts in the skeleton that sent me fleeing, even more fearful of the deadly shadows on my way down.

I ignored the building to the side of it. The busted main doors indicated probably the same treatment. Despite being visible, I stuck to the middle of the road, in the afternoon sunlight. Bright and hot, yet it did little to dispel the chill within.

Would my entire life be about fear and struggling to survive? As I passed a broken window with a stripped mannequin hanging out of it, a pang of loneliness decided to remind me that not only would my life be hard bit it would be spent alone.

Because no one was out there. Or if they were, they hid like me.

Yet, I had a small hope as I sauntered that maybe someone, who wasn't an asshole rapist or a human turned monster, would see me. Man. Woman. At this point, I'd have killed to have even a cat as a companion. I had food for it stashed near my current place. Just in case things ever got super desperate.

The afternoon light suddenly dimmed as a cloud passed over. Where had it come from?

I frowned. When I'd left there'd not been a single cloud in the sky. It was okay. The monsters still wouldn't come out.

I hoped.

My feet moved faster. I'd have to go farther.

The next block had some lower-rise buildings, only three stories. Not ideal for supplies, however, I didn't see many broken windows. The lobby doors remained closed, and locked. The panes of glass intact if dirty. I peered through them, but there wasn't enough visibility to see shit.

I pulled the door, wincing at metallic rattling. This was the part I hated.

The hammer and chisel came out of the loops from the utility belt I wore. My knapsack was for a set of clothes and essentials. I never left home without an emergency kit.

Placing the chisel against the seam with the bolt, I whacked it. Fast and hard. Don't waste time. The longer I banged, the bigger target I painted. Noise drew attention. It had been months since I'd had to fight, and I wasn't eager to break that streak. Some days I felt bad about what I had to do to Corey, but then I remembered the hungry gleam in his eye and the knife in his hand, his grin as he said, *Meat is meat.*

Humans weren't meat. When he died, I left him for the monsters. I'd eat dog food before stooping to that level.

The inside of the building felt like a tomb. Yet I doubted any of the deep pockets of shadows held any corpses. The air didn't feel of death. Nor did it appear trashed. I might have lucked out.

The apartment building I'd entered held a very standard kind of layout. Stairs going down to two basement units, the laundry and utility area for building management only. Up, I found four apartments, doors all closed. The window outside gave enough illumination to show the hallway intact. Such a good sign and a good thing, too, as that one cloud suddenly multiplied. I was losing daylight fast. I might have to hunker down somewhere and ride out the night. It wouldn't be the first time.

It saved my life more than once. My second year in, I'd gone on a recon mission for Sally, Derek, and Sloane. Got caught by a storm and spent the night in a mattress store. When I went back to our camp, it was to find them gone, only blood left behind.

As the afternoon light waned, the stairwell darkened, and I tensed, wondering if something watched me.

On the second landing, seeing more signs of locked doors, I decided I'd gone far enough. I tried the handle of the first apartment door, just in case it would cooperate.

It didn't budge. I'd have to deal with the lock. I pulled out my hammer and chisel, a girl's best friends, and made quick work of the lock. If I chose to stay here, a hardware store would provide a replacement. For tonight, I'd barricade the opening.

Bang. Bang. It took more shots than I liked to break my way in. I gave a fearful glance down the hall to the stairwell, half expecting to see a snarling face coming at me.

Nothing stirred.

I closed the door and immediately slid a small table nearby to hold it shut. I'd need heavier stuff. Something wide enough to wedge between the door and the wall a few feet in front of it. Maybe the fridge would be on wheels that worked.

My nose wrinkled as I moved from the tight entrance into the apartment. Something had died here. Not as long ago as I would have liked judging by the ripeness. It didn't bode well for scavenging, a fact reinforced by the empty cupboards. I even shone my light inside them to make sure I didn't miss anything.

Exiting the kitchen with my flashlight, the kind you could charge by shaking it hard and fast, I aimed it around and saw the signs someone had used this apartment as a base. There was litter all over. Food wrappers mostly. A toppled pile of porn magazines, stains on the couch that I didn't plan to touch.

Nothing usable jumped out of me, and I almost turned around to leave. Maybe I should find a different apartment. Maybe the person living here hadn't rifled through them all.

I should be thorough, though, hence why I went

into the bedroom and found the body. It lay on the bed, most of the decay having progressed past the wet stage. A dried husk remained that would keep evaporating over time until it was only bones.

It didn't appear as if he'd been killed, more likely died in his sleep from the drugs he took. The nightstand held a plethora of needles and pill bottles. I had a full bottle of opioids in my pack and antibiotics. Just in case.

Exiting the bedroom, I shone my light one last time around. Would I die alone like this person had? Would it be despair that got me as I finally cracked at the fact I'd never eat fast food again. I missed the Big Mac. And those crunchy salty fries. Soft serve ice cream. Unburned popcorn because it was fucking hard to make without a goddamned microwave.

The flashlight remained in my hand as I entered the hall, not bothering to close the door behind me. I aimed the beam at the next door. As I neared, I saw the signs of abuse by the handle.

I entered to find it ransacked. Along with the next.

Fuck.

I didn't realize I'd hissed it aloud until I heard it. Not as if anyone heard me. This place was long abandoned. I began to head back down the hall, to the stairs, only to pause. I hurriedly shut off my light and listened.

Creak. The noise came from the stairs, and I bolted for the nearest open apartment. I shut and leaned against the door, ear pressed to it.

At first, I heard nothing. Perhaps it was just the building shifting. Still, it didn't hurt to be cautious. I kept my cheek against the portal and had just about decided it was when safe when the hair on my body zapped to attention.

I held my breath and listened.

Huff. Huff. Grr. Ha.

Part growl, part cackle, and such bad news.

How long before it tracked me down? The door was busted and needed barricading. Possible, I thought as I glanced around. Only problem being it would leave me trapped in here.

I could confront it in the hall. My gloves meant my grip wasn't slippery on my gun. Kill it and I'd be able to use the stairs.

What if it wasn't alone?

Something brushed up against the door. A nail scratched over it, and I wanted to whimper.

It knew I was on the other side. I didn't dare move, not even to blink as I waited to see what it would do. With a thump it cackled and moved away.

I should exit now and kill it. Make my escape. Be brave.

Then my brain reminded me of the last time I fought a monster. I'd barely survived. The slash that had healed and left a thick scar throbbed in reply.

What if I could find another way out?

The window I stumbled to opened easier than expected, a piece of luck I wouldn't waste. Breathing hotly behind my mask, I slipped outside, the overcast sky still better than the shadowy apartment. My feet barely gripped the thin limestone ledge that ran decoratively around the building. Five years ago, my idea of climbing was the social ladder. Now? I was Spiderwoman without the webs.

I hoped the porous stone didn't crumble under my weight as I did my best to close the window. I couldn't get the last inch and couldn't waste time worrying about it. I inched sideways out of sight and hugged the brick, my cheek scraping against the rough surface.

Tap. Tap. Something rapped at the window I'd exited. Oh shit.

I slid over farther, breathing hard in my mask, feeling myself sweat, wishing I'd learned to pick locks. Because I had no doubt the monster found me as a result of my stupidity.

Might as well ring a fucking dinner bell. I used my anger with myself to ignore the fact I stood precariously above the ground. I had no idea where I was going or how I'd get down even. I just kept inching.

And then it happened.

The ledge cracked, and I fell.

## CHAPTER 5

THE PAST

THE PRESIDENT WENT TO MEET THE ALIEN delegation in person, despite a bunch of his advisors screaming no. Too dangerous. What if the aliens killed him or took him hostage?

The opposition party also said no, but for two reasons. One, they didn't want him to fuck it up, and two, they also didn't want him crowned in any glory.

Brokering a peace deal with aliens? The American people might just bend the rules and elect him for another term.

As for me, I didn't give a shit about the politics. This event would change the world. Who knew what wondrous things would emerge from this encounter?

Despite being at home, glued to my screen, I

dressed in my sluttiest best. I'd read a story just recently about some blue alien hottie who beamed right into someone's apartment and abducted her. They went into the stars and fell in love.

Sigh.

Unlike that heroine, though, I made sure I looked my best. Even had my makeup and hair done. Lounging on my sofa—the chenille covered in an afghan so any visitors didn't see the rips and stains—I waited with bated breath to see my first alien.

"Oh." The sound that emerged from me as the door to the spacecraft finished opening and the first visitor filled its frame. I began to understand why the gangplank was so narrow. The aliens gripped it and traversed it, seven of them in total, some treading upright, others dangling upside down as they moved.

I covered my mouth with my hand as the shock of them penetrated.

The aliens weren't cute. Or anything close to humanoid.

A good thing they claimed they came in peace, because, when those many-legged things emerged, I am pretty sure more than one person in the world screamed.

Spiders. We'd made contact with alien fucking

spiders. There went my fantasy of being kidnapped and ravished by some handsome blue-skinned ET.

The president, to his credit, remained undaunted. His staff however?

One of his male subordinates ran off. It led to a few others following him.

Probably for the best. We didn't want a diplomatic incident with the arachnids. I'd seen the movies. It didn't end well for Earth.

Gulp.

The lead spider, his limbs almost dainty and his frame colored a bright turquoise, paused in front of the president. Its mandibles flexed over its mouth, like deadly petals opening.

The president, who wore a lapel microphone, greeted the thing with a coolness that almost made me applaud.

"Welcome to the United States of America." The president held out his hand.

The spiders behind the leader tensed. I noticed the gray versions appeared to be wearing armor, and was that a bazooka strapped to the body of one?

I am pretty sure the whole fucking world held its breath next as the president, with balls of steel, waited.

Funny how even one second in a tense situation can feel as if an eternity passed.

An alien, wearing bangles, gold and silver in appearance, lifted a leg, and the cameraman had the foresight to zoom in so we could see the strange split at the end of the appendage.

They shook hands, er paw or claw? I didn't know what the fuck to call anything, but I did cry. First contact had happened in my lifetime.

Less than a week later, I cried for an even better reason.

## CHAPTER 6
THE PRESENT

As I FELL, I HAD TIME ENOUGH ONLY TO THINK, *Fuck me, this is going to hurt.* It might only be the second floor, but the impact would break something for sure.

At least I didn't see the ground coming at me, just the sun finally peeking from behind clouds. Taunting fucker.

At the last second, I closed my eyes. I hit something, but it wasn't hard ground. The object grunted and staggered but didn't drop my body.

Caught, by what? Oh shit. Shit. Shit!

I tensed and opened my eyelids, ready to scream, only to blink. It was a someone who'd managed to catch me, a male judging by his square face and stubbled jaw. He wore a knit hat over his hair and a lopsided grin.

"Hey. Nice of you to drop in." In a deep timbre, my rescuer cracked a lame joke.

He'd also saved me.

Did I say thank you? Nope. All I managed was to squeak, "Hey."

Yup. Hottest thing ever happened to me and suddenly I'm Miss Shy Girl.

"You okay?" he asked as he set me on my feet.

No. I wanted a do-over. A chance to offer him a sultry hello and thanks before bestowing a kiss on him.

Too forward?

Didn't really care. I'd been a long time without human contact. This guy didn't just represent the cake, his hunkiness was like the extra icing on top.

But did he appear overcome by my cuteness?

Nope. Then again, I wore a mask...wait a second. He didn't?

I stared at his bare mouth and uncovered nose. His lips moved. I could see them. Why didn't he wear any protective face gear? Didn't he fear the spores?

He started moving past me, and I finally started

listening to him speak. "We should go. The sun won't stay out for long."

Despite me not replying, he gripped my hand tight and tugged us into a run. Thank God one of us hadn't been addled enough to lose their survival instinct. I snapped out of my head and paid attention to the space around me.

He was right about the sun not sticking around. Clouds already scuttled to cover it. Would the gray light be enough to keep the monster inside?

My feet slapped pavement as I sprinted, and my breath huffed. On a positive note, I actually managed to keep pace with him. Gone was the flabby girl who did yoga twice a month and thought herself fit. Now I had abs. Biceps. Triceps. All the 'eps because with nothing to do but hide and read, I kept in shape.

My savior appeared to know where he wanted to go, turning a few times until we reached a tall building, the windows on the main floor boarded over. The signs above, while dirty, boasted a coffee shop and a pharmacy. What I wouldn't give for a latte with a dusting of cinnamon on top.

He was more interested in the shattered front doors between the stores. We entered a tight lobby, full of shadows.

To my surprise, he pulled something out and shook it. He had a flashlight just like mine. It created a soft glowing light.

I glanced over my shoulder. Had we been followed by the monster? Picked up by a new threat? I wasn't sure where we were other than far from my home.

The dude in the hat walked toward a door, saying nothing at all. Should I leave or follow the guy in the long duster? Could he get any sexier?

He held open the door to the stairs, only then meeting my gaze. He arched a brow noticing I hadn't moved. "Coming?"

That kind of depended on him.

"I don't know you," was what I replied, though.

"You know enough to realize I am not the type to let you die needlessly."

"You could be the type to kidnap women for torture." Yup, that came out of my mouth. Accused him of being a sociopath.

He laughed, showing off beautiful teeth, all the better for nibbling me with. "What if instead I'm just a nice guy who happened to save a beautiful woman?"

"Okay, now you're putting it on thick," I grumbled, cheeks hot but secretly pleased. I headed for him. "You should have stopped at nice guy," I added as I drew even.

"I doubt you'll think I'm nice in a few minutes. How do you feel about stairs?"

Seven flights later, huffing and puffing, I hated them with a passion, especially since hot dude appeared unruffled. I, on the other hand, leaned on the wall and tried to not die.

"It's not much farther," he remarked.

"Ha,." I croaked.

"It occurs to me, I haven't introduced myself. Xavion."

He would have a sexy name. Me? "Cecilia." And I swear, if he starting singing the Simon and Garfunkel song that made my mother name me, I would hit him, cute or not! Growing up, I'd heard the many versions of "Cecilia" at every major event in my life. Hearing it now might make me snap.

"Cecilia." He mulled over my name, rolling it off his tongue and lips like a fine wine.

"And you're Xavion what?" He'd not mentioned a last name.

He smiled again. "Just Xavion. The one and only in the world. Just like you are the very last and first Cecilia."

Because I like embarrassing myself, I blurted out, "Xavion and Cecilia, the new Adam and Eve."

## CHAPTER 7

THE PAST

THE PRESIDENT DIDN'T GET SICK RIGHT AWAY. Or if he did, he hid it from everyone. No one noticed, at first, that the group that met the aliens disappeared from public view. Everyone focused on the ET's in our midst.

The aliens were given an abandoned embassy in the nation's capital. Diplomatic ties with that particular country had been severed a while back due to election meddling in 2020, and not by the two superpowers always in the news.

The aliens moved in, and the president had the embassy heavily guarded. No protesting was tolerated and got shut down before it started.

The media screamed about the constitution. The

president told them to fuck off and not start a galactic war.

America actually approved.

The spaceship was cordoned off; however, scientists were given access by the visitors. It didn't run any mechanics or physics that made any sense to humanity but would revolutionize the world. Or so I heard on the internet.

I was glued to every single broadcast involving the aliens. What did they eat? Some weird paste stuff that they grew on their ship. Heavy on the protein apparently. They kept a day and night schedule. Spoke in clicks that were already being learned by an AI system for real-time communication.

The world spent those first few weeks in a celebration, which might be why the news took us all by surprise.

It was an alien who died first.

We didn't know that though. The world might be watching the live, twenty-four-hour footage of the embassy, but we saw little from the outside, only what the government released.

When we finally did find out, it was to discover the spiders weren't faring well. The body of the first dead one was brought back to the ship and a new person on board took their place. The next body was given to human scientists, because, by the end of week three since their arrival, the president appeared to be ill and two of those there for the landing had died. It led to all those at the first meeting being taken into custody for observation.

The aliens were put under strict quarantine and the ship under a military watch with orders to fire if they saw anything hinky.

Illegal drone footage—achieved by launching dozens at a time in the hopes of getting one good video—began to emerge showing the embassy court-yard with the spiders spending more time outside. Basking in the sun. Each day looking weaker and duller, their carapaces turning an ashy gray.

The president died. The vice president took over even as he appeared sick. The illness was spreading.

Hospitals soon became overrun with the sick. Morgues couldn't handle all the bodies. The survival rate proved small, and of those who beat the plague, reports came out of strange violent behavior.

They called the airborne illness Arachvid-1. It would seem despite all the evidence to the contrary, aliens and humans were incompatible. Their very existence poisoned the air and made us sick.

Which led to the murder of the remaining aliens and the scuttling of their ship. Not that I cared, by that point. I'd locked myself in. Barricaded my door. Hoarded my food even as I wanted to eat all of it.

I watched the broadcasts and videos of the world dying. Arachcvid-1 had a ninety-five percent fatality. But those who survived were changed.

People tried to protect themselves from it. We pulled out our COVID-19 masks from the 2020 pandemic.

It didn't stop the spread. Even more died as riots rocked the streets and despair killed those who thought suicide would be kinder.

Had I any drugs I might have been tempted to chug them.

Instead, I hid inside my safe cave, watching my food pile dwindle, glued to the internet until the day I lost the signal. I didn't dare venture forth even as my supplies dwindled.

I feared what happened outside.

Two weeks into my self-isolation, the almost constant sirens stopped. The days and weeks following, I'd hear engines outside and the occasional screams.

A thump at my door had me muffling my whimpers with a fist in my mouth. I wanted to wake up from the nightmare. Instead, I ran out of food.

Hunger forced me out of my comfort zone.

I layered on my gear. Mask, face shield, hat over my ears, jacket, pants, all taped around the cuffs. I waddled out, made it to the lobby level, and looked out onto the results of a civil apocalypse. Burned wrecks. Garbage in the streets. And a body lying splayed on the sidewalk.

Oh God, a dead body.

I went flying up the stairs, panting and sobbing behind my mask, snotting up so badly, I yanked it free. My tears made it impossible to see as I headed up the third flight of stairs to my floor.

As I stepped through the door for my landing, a hand went over my mouth, calloused and painful. Another hand grabbed me and shoved me face first against the wall.

A low voice muttered, "Pretty pussy. Pretty pussy. Scream for me."

Terrifying, especially since he grinded against me. I knew what he planned.

Would I let him do it? Maybe if I didn't fight, he wouldn't hurt me?

Like fuck. I found my lady balls and stomped his foot. He yelled and then gasped as threw my elbow back and slammed his diaphragm. Thank God I'd taken a few self-defense lessons. When I whirled, I swung my satchel while screaming nonstop.

I'm pretty sure that my unhinged behavior, and not my feeble blows, sent my assailant running.

Shaken, I went to my apartment and did not to creep out again until I ran out of everything edible—spices, salt, even the vinegar was gone before I dared. In one hand I had a kitchen knife. And as for my throat? I tried not to swallow my courage.

## CHAPTER 8

THE PRESENT

"How much further?" I asked as we passed a landing with a giant nine painted on a door.

"Just one more set," Xavion said.

"I thought you weren't trying to kill me," I huffed, slowly trudging up the next step.

"I'm not."

"Doesn't seem that way," I grumbled.

"Trust me."

Trust a stranger I'd just met? Who saved my life?

Why not? It wasn't as if I had other plans. He was also the first non-crazy person I'd seen in a while.

Here was to hoping he didn't plan to have me for dinner later. As in slice me and dice me. I'd met a cannibal once. A cute one, who had sex with me for a month before he tried to make me into a meal.

Needless to say, we broke up when I killed him.

"We needed to go this high to find a level untouched by the scavengers," he stated, holding open the door for the tenth floor.

Which was something I knew from my own excursions. People went for the easy marks first. I was guilty of the same. As supplies grew sparse, I learned to be more fit. Just not fit enough to do that many floors so fast.

"Have you been living here long?" I asked, wondering if it was safe now to remove my own mask. Xavion didn't seem bothered.

"A few weeks. I moved once I've cleared an area."

"Cleared it of what?"

"Monsters."

Pretty sure he didn't refer to the first type of monster I ever met, the wannabe rapist. "Do you mean mutants?" I asked to clarify.

Remember how some humans survived the virus but changed? I might have forgotten to mention they didn't turn into zombies but some freaky, mutant version of a person and a spider.

Hideous, as you can imagine. Mandibles poking from human lips. Eyes multi-faceted. Fingers fused.

And gooey.

"Mutants. Monsters. Same thing."

"You hunt them on purpose?" The very idea seemed...nuts. "You have a death wish?"

His lips twitched. "More like the less there are, the safer it becomes for everyone."

"Have you met other people?" In some of my fantasies I stumbled across a trove of human survivors. They'd have figured out how to restart society. To make flour and bread and how to grow things without killing them.

"Yes."

"And?" His one syllable answer didn't satisfy.

"And most of them were a lot less trusting than you."

A dig about me being dumb? I couldn't tell, and he had turned from me to enter a door he'd just opened. No lock. Then again, what was the point if he wasn't home?

Entering, I was struck by how normal the place looked. Tile floor from the entrance leading into the kitchen. A breakfast bar overlooking a large open living room space and, at the far end, a bank of windows overlooking the city.

"You don't cover your windows!" I exclaimed. He had kept the flashlight shaken and illuminated our whole trip up.

"I'm usually out hunting the monsters at night. Besides, they hunt more by sound than sight or even scent."

I had to ask. "Why don't you wear a mask outside?"

"Why do you bother?" he countered.

"The plague—"

"Has already infected you. Everyone on the planet got it."

I shook my head. "Did not. Obviously, or we wouldn't be talking." I almost rolled my eyes.

"Oh, you got it all right. A mask can't stop it. Nothing can. It's in the air. It's on our skin. In the water we drink."

"I think I'd have noticed if I'd gotten sick. I'm neither dead or one of those *things*." My lip curled.

"There is a third outcome."

My brain, which had wondered about it before, had my lips saying, "Immunity."

## CHAPTER 9

PAST TO PRESENT.

I KNEW FROM THE NEWS REPORTS JUST HOW deadly the virus could be. I'd seen it when the internet still worked. But I had hoped that those of us who managed to stay alive would be better than the movies. Better than the books about the apocalypse.

Surely, we wouldn't become a world of Mad Maxes.

I was so wrong.

There was something ironic about the fact that, of the few who survived, the lucky ones just had to be the sort who didn't mind meting out violence. Why wasn't it ever the kind and gentle souls who survived the apocalypse and restarted society?

Because goodness doesn't have the cold lack of empathy to survive.

I learned after my first assault that being nice hurt. I also learned Lady Macbeth was right. The bloody spots never came out.

I killed. The survivors I encountered left me no choice. Given my lack of skill, it was often bloody, noisy, and messy since I always cried, snotted, and puked.

Having lady balls didn't mean I lacked a heart.

Things could have been different for those I had to murder. They just needed to respect the fact I had a right to safety and liberty. History likes to repeat itself, and women always did get the brunt.

There was a spot of good news though. The most depraved didn't live long past the first and second year. The problem with being an asshole to every-one? At one point, someone got tired of it.

Like the guy who called himself El Raido. He captured me and Katia. When I saw what he did to her, I had already readied myself for my turn. He never suspected, and the pen jabbed him in the neck before he flung me off.

I hit the floor so hard I bit my tongue bloody. El Raido staggered, hand to the pen. No blood.

That didn't start spraying until he yanked out the pen holding it in.

I looked like that girl in the movie after the bucket of blood dumped on her. I emerged, and his thugs thought I was a monster.

Good if it meant they left me alone.

As the worst despots in the city died and their henchmen drifted off to other neighborhoods, the people I ran into tended to be more decent—even the cannibal until that final fatal act.

I made a few friends the first few years of the apocalypse. Some only casually. Fitting in somewhere wasn't easy. It turned out that sometimes I preferred being alone. Especially when the group didn't divide things equally. The leader? He didn't go out. He stayed inside with his two concubines and expected us to bring him back the goods.

For what? Why should I scrounge for people who meant nothing to me?

Sharing wasn't something anyone did well anymore making Xavion's decision to take me to his lair a big deal. I noticed that while nothing locked on the way in, he did secure his apartment door, even wedged a chair under the handle. Once he'd reassured himself we were safe, he offered me a sealed bottle of water.

Clean. Water.

It had to be a dream. It was also a distraction. "You didn't answer my question. Are we immune to the plague?"

"I am."

I put my hand to my face shield. "Meaning you don't know for sure about me."

"You must be immune too. Masks don't do shit."

"What makes you think I'm not a mutant?"

He grinned. "If you are, then you're the sexiest one thus far."

"I could be hideous under this thing."

"You have gorgeous eyes."

"Flatterer," I grumbled. Then, before I could change my mind, I peeled the mask off my face. Licked my lips.

"Nice to see you have an actual mouth." He stared at my lips.

Would it be wrong to say, all the better to eat you with? I almost missed the bottle he tossed my way. I barely caught it. Unscrewing the lid, I guzzled the water. Stale. Warm. I didn't care. What came out of the pipes these days lacked the clarity of the days when city workers ran the filters and pumps.

Only when I was done did I realize he'd moved

into the kitchen proper, opening cupboards, laying out a feast, not just of packaged expired food.

"Are those vegetables?" I honed in on the sight and ran my finger over the long thick cucumber.

His voice emerged gruff as he said, "Yes. There's a place outside the city that trades once a month or so. Even in winter."

"You've left the city?" Color me even more surprised. "What's it like?"

"Not as many mutants compared to here. The big wide-open spaces mean less spots for them to hide in the daytime."

Less, not none, meaning it still had its dangers.

"Isn't it a long walk?" I asked. The gas for cars stopped working a long time ago.

"Why would I walk when I can cycle?"

The moment he said it I could have slapped myself. It never even occurred to me. I was one of those people who didn't care for bicycles back in the day, an opinion only got worse given the number of times I almost got run over on the sidewalk.

I freely admit to mocking those with their bullet helmets and intense expressions. Don't even get me started on men in those spandex shorts.

"Is it a long trip by bike?"

"To get past suburbia? A few hours, especially since you can't go direct."

He didn't want people following him.

I could respect that. "Are things better for us outside the city?"

He hesitated before replying. "Not so much better as different."

"Different how?" I pulled out my knife and sliced the cucumber.

"In the city, you can scavenge for supplies. Clothing. Food. Weapons. You just need to find a place that hasn't been stripped." Given how fast people had croaked, there was a lot of good stuff left lying around.

But even I knew— "It's not an endless supply."

He shook his head. "It isn't."

Was it wrong to drool when he brought out some vinegar and dill to shake on it?

The first tangy bite almost made me cry.

We were both quiet as I ate most of the plate. He had a few slices and mostly watched me.

"If it's less dangerous and you can get fresh food outside the city, why live here?" I asked.

"Shit's not free. So I scavenge for stuff and hunt monsters."

I shuddered. "You're braver than me. I avoid them."

"You survived this long. I'd say you're just as courageous."

That made me snort, and then I couldn't stop. If he only knew how scared I was most of the time.

"How did you find me?" I asked when I finally calmed down.

"By accident. I was scouting out a spot for tonight's raid when I saw you coming out of the window."

"You're lucky I didn't crush you."

"Ha, you'd have to be a lot heavier, Lia."

He'd shortened my name, and I didn't mind it.

I eyed him. The food. "Why are you being so nice to me?"

His grin held a hint of mischief as he said, "Earlier you called us Adam and Eve. We both know where they ended up." And then, in case I was dense, he spelled it out. "Naked in bed."

## CHAPTER 10

HE SAID IT. OUT LOUD. THE THING I'D THOUGHT since meeting Xavion but not vocalized. He just tossed it out there, the fact he wanted us to have sex.

I blushed and stammered. "I barely know you."

"Hence why we're talking."

Good point. Also, since when did I care about how long I knew a guy? Wouldn't be the first time I'd met a stranger and screwed them. This was the apocalypse. No such thing as a one-night stand, only missed opportunities.

"How do I know you're not a cannibal?"

His nose wrinkled. "Not big on land meat. But I do like fish. Since you're not a mermaid, I think you're safe."

"Do you run a gang? Are you going to tie me up

and sell me? Is your last girlfriend locked up somewhere?"

Once I started asking, I couldn't stop. He laughed as he replied, "I'm a loner who doesn't believe in bondage."

"What about the girlfriend?" I asked, my tone light and teasing.

"I don't have one. Yet."

Oh yes, he stared at me as he said the last bit.

It was sexy, which might be why my clumsy ass just about tackled him.

The guy knew how to brace. Xavion handled me hitting him, and while my hands curled around his neck—in an almost death grip born of desperate need —his arms came around me and held me just as tight.

Thank fuck because I might have cried if he'd rejected me.

I didn't realize how much I missed—needed— human contact until that very moment. Holding another person, being held, could mean so much.

We kissed, which sounded so trite.

It was more than that. It was two people coming together in a clash of lips and teeth, our panting breaths comingling, our hands clutching, bodies grinding.

He groaned into my mouth.

Sexy as hell.

He moaned again when I tongued the seam of his lips, urging him to part them.

It surprised me that he let me take the lead. Thus far he'd been brash. Very macho alpha male.

But in this...he seemed more than content to let me explore at my pace. I devoured him. Tested and tasted his tongue and mouth. Inhaled his hums of pleasure and purred my own.

It made my knees literally weak, and I sagged in his arms. His hands slid to my ass and held me upright. As I began to lose myself to the pleasure, his turn came to dominate.

He kept our mouths locked as he lifted me and carried me to the bedroom. It had a thick pile of blankets that smelled of the outdoors still, where he'd obviously washed them. On to that plush bed he laid me and stood staring.

I gazed right back, my lids heavy and shuttering half of my eyes.

His mouth opened, and I expected something dirty.

Hot.

"Are you sure you want to do this?"

Sensitivity? If I'd had something in my hand I'd have whacked him with it for ruining the moment.

"After that Frenching, do you really have to ask?" Yeah, I snapped, frustration coiling in my panties.

His lips quirked. "Would you rather I just took?"

I arched a brow. "I'd prefer if you used that mouth for something other than yapping."

My hand slid to my pants, my thumb hooking the waistband and tugging in case I'd not hinted hard enough.

He grabbed my ankle, and I gasped. His fingers curled around the hem of my pant, both legs, and he smiled. I lifted my ass to shimmy them down, and he yanked them free.

It should be noted my underwear was clean, but functional. G-strings sucked if you got sweaty with nerves.

He didn't seem to mind my waist-high briefs. He palmed me, and I bit my lip as I arched into the touch.

"Guess fair is fair." He stripped out his coat first, tossing it onto a chair across from the bed. Then his shirt.

Oh sweet heaven on Earth. My poor panties would never dry.

He had the leanest, meanest body I'd ever had the pleasure of seeing. No fat on him. Abs I wanted to touch. A vee I wanted to explore.

A smoldering expression on his face as he suddenly covered my body with his own. My thighs spread, welcoming his hard body. Even through the material of his jeans, I could feel his hardness. No doubting he wanted me.

I loosely locked my legs around him, drawing him close, lifting my hips to grind against him.

He obliged, rubbing me in a way that drew a gasp and had me grabbing for the comforter in my fisted hands.

He hummed his pleasure and then nipped at my tongue when my hands slid over his flesh and ended with my nails digging into the muscles of his back.

"Fuck me," he muttered against my mouth, and I knew he was close to losing control.

That made two of us.

I grabbed at my own jacket, got caught trying to remove it, and needed his help.

It should have been awkward. It turned out hot and sexy, as he touched me all over as he helped strip me. With my shirt gone, he braced himself on one arm so his other hand could skim over my belly. His fingers traced the skin leading to my breast. He squeezed and cupped, kneaded it as his callused fingers found my nipple. He tweaked it. Rolled it.

Dipped his head to catch an erect nipple with his lips.

Oh hell yeah. I arched, thrusting it against his mouth. Making my pleasure known. He sucked my areola, even gently bit.

He switched sides and did it again. I bit my lip lest I cry out.

He did it again.

I groaned. "Xavion." I didn't even realize my fingers dug into his scalp and tugged at his hair. My need had me mindless.

I wanted to come. For the pleasure to never stop.

I needed him.

I shoved at him until he raised himself high enough I could reach for his pants. He had to adjust his position to assist, but at least he didn't argue.

They unbuttoned easily enough, and then I was shoving at them, stopping only when his dick, going commando, popped into view.

Damn.

He got worried because I stared at it.

"You okay?" he asked.

Better than okay. It was like Christmas morning.

The dick of all dicks.

"If you ask me one more time, I will finish myself off while you watch."

Which might actually be more torturous for me.

At least he didn't need any more encouragement.

His hands gripped my thighs. Parted them. He fingered the edge of my panties, touching the edge of my lip. He decided to torture me by placing a kiss on my leg above my knee. Then higher.

He blew on me. Hot enough, and hard enough, I felt it and cried out. "Damn you, stop teasing me."

Over me he appeared, his arms braced on either side. The head of his dick nudged, and he stared at me. I stared right back, until he starting pushing into me. Then my head tilted, and I sighed at the stretch.

The pulse.

The connection inside me.

His lips found mine as he sank even deeper, nudging me in that special spot that hitched my breath. I clung to him. Clawed him when he gave a bump and hit me good in my special spot. My hips tilted, inviting him deeper.

He took it slow. Grinding at me in a way that held me on orgasm's edge. My body tensed. Wanted. And he teased.

"Give it to me," I demanded.

"Fuck," he uttered into my mouth as he pumped me, faster and faster, the friction, the stretch, the bump...

When my orgasm hit, my mouth opened wide, and it would have been an epic scream if I'd had the breath to eject it.

My whole body exploded with pleasure. I went rigid, my mind blank. It must have been uncomfortable when I clamped down super hard on his dick.

He liked it.

Hot spurts and the deep pulsing of his cock showed him coming, and then like a man, he collapsed on top of me.

I didn't mind. I hugged him and reveled in how he struggled to catch his breath, his face buried in the crook of my neck and shoulder.

"Shit. I must be squishing you," he finally said. Keeping our bodies joined, he managed to roll so I lay on top of him.

I was okay with that. Especially when I pushed up and his semihard dick still inside me gave me a pleasurable jolt.

He groaned.

I grinned. "Don't tell me you're done for the night." Bold, but I was feeling pretty good after epic sex. "You know, my dildo never lets me down."

But it lacked that one thing that made the orgasm better. Companionship.

"Who said I was done?" He thrust up into me. Already harder than before.

"Well, I never did find out how old you are. Could be a man your age needs time to recover."

"Are you daring me to fuck you?"

"Yes." I couldn't help but grin as I ground myself against him.

He got bigger.

And that climax of before? Good, but already I craved another.

I rode him, slowly rotating my hips, tits out so that he could play with them.

Cowgirl was a nice position for control. I knew where I wanted the tip of his dick grinding. And for added fun, his tweaks of my nipples gave me extra jolts.

He stared at me as I rode, my hips rocking and rolling against him. I could tell his excitement level by how tense his jaw went and how his expression smoldered.

I bit my lip as I continued to ride, clenching him tight. Staring at him as I came.

Feeling a connection that shook me to the core.

My turn to collapse in a boneless heap on him.

He held me, hand stroking my back.

Saying nothing.

Which was good, because he probably would have ruined it.

And I so wanted to bask in what it felt like to be happy.

He, on the other hand, cursed. "Fuck me! I forgot to reset the traps." Because he'd ben distracted.

By me.

As I watched his naked ass bolt for the door, I smiled. I could get used to this.

## CHAPTER 11

For the first time in forever, I slept cuddled in someone's arms. Woke to Xavion lightly kissing my shoulder.

I shoved him. "Ew. Way too sticky. I need to wash first."

He chuckled. "Fair enough. How does a shower sound?"

Say what? Most water coming out of pipes these days was dirty. It required filtering to even drink. Clean water meant putting out buckets and hauling them. Despite the effort, I fetched enough water to washcloth myself a few times a week.

But Xavion didn't have a bucket. He had a shower.

"There's no hot water," he said, "but lucky for us,

this building actually had a rooftop cistern. It's still collecting and dispensing."

As if I cared. I welcomed the cold water and the soap. I'd not had a proper cleanse since the last rainstorm when I'd stood on a rooftop shivering, hoping I didn't get killed because I wanted shampooed hair.

Today, I didn't shower alone, and even better, I enjoyed a morning sausage. First the dick kind, then an actual hunk of meat.

"Where did you find this?" I asked as he handed me some salted jerky. The store-bought kind had long expired and gone rancid.

"Made it," he admitted with pride.

"From an animal?" It occurred to me I'd only seen one type of living creature.

Seeing my face, he laughed. "Yes, an animal!"

"Is it rat?" I'd always been taught they and cockroaches would be the only things that would survive the apocalypse.

"It's rabbit. The ones immune to the plague have been multiplying like crazy. Lack of predators in the wild has been helping."

I loved bunnies. In the olden days, I would never eat one. Protein, though. I bit into the jerky and felt happy. "I thought you were a fish man."

"Mostly. But I'm also practical. This salts easier and doesn't take up much room."

It was salty and delicious, as was his cum because I later did something I didn't do for many guys.

But he was special. He made me feel special. Happy.

After the sex, he showed me the building and the security he'd built in. When we'd come up the stairs, I'd assumed he had almost none, other than the brace on the stairwell door. After all, the apartment was left open. What I didn't see was the threads he'd placed over some entrances. Subtle and yet clever.

He'd barricaded ventilation shafts. Created a noisy curtain over the elevator opening. As for the stairway, in case they made it past the main floor to ours, he showed me the bucket he kept over it.

"What's in it?" I asked.

"Oil."

"How did we not knock it over last night?"

"The bucket is for when I'm in residence. When I leave, I put the thread over the door. If someone opens it, the thread I crazy glue over the seam snaps." He pointed to the remains. They seemed like a cobweb.

"I never noticed yesterday." Then again, I'd been

out of breath and eager to stop climbing by that point.

"And I doubt the mutants will either, or any survivors that come poking."

"I just kept my door locked," I admitted. Only once did I get a visitor who insisted with an axe on coming in. A so-called human. I did the world a favor and made sure he wouldn't repopulate.

"How often do you go out scouting?" he asked.

"I try to stock up for a month or more at a time. For winter, I usually make sure the building I've found has a few apartments still loaded with stuff."

"How often do you leave the city?"

I hesitated before admitting, "I don't."

He didn't blink before saying, "You've made yourself a prisoner."

Feeling discomfited, I blurted out, "I don't take unnecessary risk. How often do you leave your safe place?"

"Every day."

My turn to gape. "Isn't that tempting danger?"

"More like courting it. I wasn't kidding when I said I hunted the mutants. So long as they exist, we will never be safe."

"You can't really think you can kill them all?"

"No, but I can try."

"Wouldn't it just be easier to move away? You said the country is pretty good."

"Yes, but the raw supplies are still mostly in the city. Ordinary people shouldn't have to risks their lives to access them."

"So you risk yours?" I noticed how he didn't think of himself as ordinary. Then again, anyone who actively sought out mutants probably was a whole different level.

"Someone should. Besides, it's not as if I'm that important." He shrugged. "No family to care."

I almost opened my mouth to say I cared, and stopped. I'd known him a day.

As we headed back up the hall, I glanced back at the bucket. "How does the oil help? Is it for tracking?"

"Setting them on fire."

I gaped as he entered the apartment.

Savage. And yet, could I really say anything? Our lives hung in the balance.

"Lunch?" he asked as I entered. He held out something that claimed to be spray cheese and a box of crackers. The paste was processed orange salty goo that in my healthier days I would have turned up my nose at.

I groaned and moaned eating it.

Best lunch ever.

After our meal—and the sex for dessert—he dressed and strapped on some weapons. I remained in a T-shirt and panties.

"Where are you going?" It would be dark in a few hours.

"Hunting. Want to come?""

"Hunt mutants?" My eyes widened. I shook my head.

That first day, I let him go alone. Once night hit, I paced. Worried. Ranted. Railed.

Xavion returned dirty but alive. I pounced him, so happy he'd come back.

When he left the following day, I joined him, insisting I didn't want to fight but could act as a lookout. I didn't want to be alone and wondering.

I put on my stealth gear, including weapons, but when it came to the mask, I held it out and chewed my lower lip. Subconsciously I'd known for a while I'd probably developed an immunity to the plague. Yet, I'd been afraid. I was tired of living like that. The mask went into my pocket.

Off we went, side by side, him alert but attentive to me, showing off the places he'd cleared. A few held a lingering stench of smoke. He taught me how to see signs of buildings that had mutant activity.

The monsters didn't usually use the front door, and once I looked in the right places, I could spot their presence. He let me track the block after that lesson, and I led us into an alley and a metal door pried open. Entering the kitchen of a fast food restaurant that would never serve burgers again, he immediately sought a way down into the basement below, where he dispatched a pair of monsters hiding behind the boiler.

I watched him do it. The brave knight facing off against the hissing beasts. He was poetry in motion, using a sword in a way that proved it wasn't just an accessory to his outfit.

It was so fucking hot we had sex on the counter that used to serve drinks and the bar food.

It became a pattern for us. Hunt by day, returning by twilight, locking up and having wild sex.

Sometimes we made it to the bedroom. Other times, I ended up back against a wall, a leg around his hips as he fucked me.

We both came each time. Flesh to flesh. No pulling out. No condom. And years since I'd taken birth control.

I didn't care. I'd been resigned to spending my life alone. Now I had Xavion and plenty of morning-after pills. Every few days, I took an expired one. I wasn't dumb enough to want to get pregnant.

Not yet. But for the first time in a long time, I could see a future...with Xavion.

He taught me that I'd been barely surviving. I learned to properly fight. Hand to hand, and with a knife. He took me blocks away to practice firing a gun on top of a roof in full daylight.

I'd not realize it the first night, but he showed me later on, that he never took a direct route home. Just in case we were followed.

We didn't just kill mutants, though. We accumulated supplies. Canned food. Rice. Pasta. Those latter two lasted a long time if kept dry. Sugar and spices. Salt being important in the making of jerky he informed me.

It was the romantic apocalypse I'd fantasized about. The last man and woman on earth finding each other and falling in love.

I should have known we'd eventually hit the part in the movie where bad shit happens. I just never expected it to happen while we were in bed at home.

## CHAPTER 12

THERE WAS SOMETHING HEINOUS ABOUT BEING accosted in a place I considered safe. Especially since we'd had a successful forage the day before. Three more mutants down, probably a million more to go, but Xavion wasn't daunted.

We'd come back with a mother lode that had us dragging a pair of large suitcases on wheels. A little noisier than usual but the sun was out, the monsters in bed, and I was in love. Especially since he offered to carry my suitcase up those ten flights of stairs.

I didn't let him, of course, but the fact he treated me like someone special had me ripping off his clothes the moment we stumbled into the apartment.

We had sex. Then we made love and, in a pool of

late afternoon sunlight, spilling onto the bed, fell asleep.

The drool on my cheek woke me.

Instinct kicked in, and I screamed as I rolled. As I hit the floor, I heard a boom. I shut my eyes and covered my ears. Told myself to wake up. This had to be a nightmare.

Only when Xavion said, "Lia," did I peek over the edge of the mattress.

Xavion remained under our nest of blankets, spattered in mutant goo and carcass. He folded the sheets back over the corpse as he rose. Naked, lean, yummy.

Some might wonder that my mind could jump in so many directions at once; fear, fight, lust. Welcome to the apocalypse.

Once more, we'd defied death. I wanted to celebrate, but Xavion didn't seem to share my enthusiasm.

"Get dressed. We need to go."

"Can't we just dump the sheets?" I eyed the mess. "Maybe swap the mattress too."

"We can't stay. They know our location."

They obviously being the mutants. "You think there's more?" Sometimes they traveled in groups.

But with one down, and the two of us working together... "We can handle it."

"Two, three, even four, probably. But why take the chance?"

Leave? It shouldn't have given me such a pang. How many homes had I gone through since the apocalypse?

Still... It made me sad. "Can't we just set a trap and kill any of its buddies that come looking?"

He cast me a look that said don't be stupid.

"You can't expect us to move at night?" Night had fallen while we napped.

Rather than reply, I saw him looking at the arm sticking out from under the sheet.

"Fuck," he muttered.

"What's wrong?"

"It's got some kind of marking." He pointed to the scarring on its forearm. Swirls and whorls.

"And?"

"Reminds me of something a guy passing through said a few months ago. Claimed he'd come across mutants banding together and using scar tattoos to show what clan they belonged to. Apparently, some of these groups are seeking out humans for sport."

"That would imply them thinking and strategizing."

He didn't reply.

"Wait a second. These things are mindless monsters." It was what helped me mentally when I had to kill one.

"Most are, but I've encountered some that can comprehend my words. Even reply."

I snorted. "Now you're shitting me." The mutants were much like zombies in film. Mindless, moaning, and snapping beasts.

"Don't tell me you're that surprised. Five years ago, they were all people. That knowledge, that memory is still in there somewhere."

"If this is supposed to evoke sympathy, it's failing."

"Fuck no. They're murderous beasts who will torture and eat you. Never hesitate. Just saying don't underestimate them."

"I wasn't planning to," was my dry reply.

"Glad to hear it, because the guy also said the ones with tattoo might share a hive mind."

Worse and worse. I growled. "So they are the Borg." Or given they arrived in a sphere and not a cube, they should have a different name like Sphorg.

"I don't know if it's true, but just in case, we

should move before they come looking. Get dressed, armed, and be ready to go in three minutes."

"Three?" No point in arguing. The carcass on the bed kept any stupid words in check. If the guy who hunted monsters for sport said, move your ass, then I really should move my ass.

I ran for the bathroom. Speed peed, brushed my teeth, and dressed in less than a minute and a half. Then I strapped on my weapons.

Xavion was in the kitchen packing a knapsack with food. Mine bulged already on the counter beside a sword and a rifle.

"There's a long barrel. You know how to use it?" We'd developed a comfortable camaraderie that held much sarcasm and teasing.

His grin held naughty male satisfaction as he said, "You would know. Three times was it this morning?"

How could he still make me blush?

I slung the knapsack on my arm and followed him to the door and saw where we'd made our mistake. It gaped wide open.

"Fuck me, we didn't lock it." He scrubbed his face and guilt oozed from him. Securing the door and apartment was usually his job when we got home. However, in this case, it was technically my fault. I'd distracted him with a blowjob the moment we walked in.

"Sorry." I hung my head, my cheeks burning.

"Don't be. Even if we had locked it, the mutant would have been in the hallway or stairwell waiting for us."

"You know a lot about the mutants," I said as he opened the door and peeked out.

"Didn't have much else to think about once the world ended."

"Are you bitter the people in charge were so dumb? I mean, why did they have to meet on Earth? They should have done it in a space station, where once shit hit the fan, they could have blown it up." I railed against the misfortune.

He rolled his shoulders. "Wouldn't have mattered if they did it in space. The plague required sunlight to trigger. The UV rays mixed with the alien spider pheromones created a pathogen that couldn't be filtered from the air. Some people proved more susceptible than others."

"Why are we immune?" I asked as we reached the stairwell.

"Because, according to Darwin, only the fittest survive." He would, of course, say that with a cocky grin. I couldn't help but smile back because I was one of those surviving.

Up yours, Darwin.

The stairs had a smell to them that had Xavion hesitating rather than going down. His lips pressed close to my ear as he muttered, "We can't go down."

I wasn't about to argue; however, I did wonder his plan as he grabbed the bucket and spilled it on the landing before we climbed.

I wanted to ask why we were going up, too far up to escape down to street level, unless you had wings. I didn't have wings, or a rope. Just a blind faith in the guy holding my hand.

At the top was when he pulled out a lighter and a cigarette. I almost asked him since when did he smoke. He lit and dropped the cigarette, and my eyes widened in understanding. The whoosh below confirmed his strategy. He'd made the stairwell an impassable inferno for mutants. Which sounded good until I realized he'd trapped us on the rooftop in the dark.

I didn't like it very much. This was nothing like the time he'd woken me early and dragged me up here at his insistence. In a comforter, we'd snuggled and watched the cresting dawn. The moment its warm rays hit us, I'd turned my face into it. Enjoyed it. Felt compelled to admit, *"I spent three years avoiding sunshine."*

Because everyone said the sun triggered the plague. Made it worse. True and false.

To the aliens it proved deadly, and it activated the virus that plagued humanity. However, afterwards, the mutated suffered in its rays. Like vampires, only not the sexy kind.

Smoke leached from the edges of the door. The fire had caught. How far would it burn? It might fizzle out. Either way, we couldn't stay up here forever.

"Once we hit the street, we will have to move fast," Xavion explained.

"You do realize we're twelve stories up?" I reminded in case he'd forgotten.

"I know. But we can't stay here."

"I don't suppose we could wait until the dawn?" The night wasn't meant for humans to roam.

"Depends. How do you like living?"

"Ugh." My fantasy life was coming to an end.

But at least I still had Xavion.

"Come on, Lia, it's not that bad. They haven't won yet." He held out his hand, one leg bent, foot resting on the ledge.

"Is this where you admit you're actually a

mutant who can fly?" Spoken as I walked toward him. Better the hunk I knew than the spider mutant who wanted to eat my face.

His fingers were firm and reassuring around mine. "I'll keep you safe. Ready?"

For anything.

## CHAPTER 13

KNOWING WE WERE GOING DOWN AND HOW IT would happen? Two different things. The dark rooftop didn't reveal many options. Did Xavion have a ladder stashed? Maybe a fire escape that I'd never seen since we usually approached from the front, not the back where he peered down.

Somehow, I had previously missed the fact there was a contraption holding a window-washing scaffold to the ledge. It wobbled as Xavion helped me on to it.

"How long has this thing been here?" I muttered.

"Long enough to save us."

Good point. I tried to be more grateful and dug my nails into my palms when he cranked something and the suspended scaffold jolted into motion.

"Is it a bad time to admit I'm scared of heights?" I stared straight ahead, not down.

"Are you more scared of heights or mutants?"

"I'd really prefer a third option," I muttered, clutching the bar tight as the contraption jerked and squealed as it cranked down slowly.

"Did you put this thing in place for an emergency escape?" I asked, anything to forget the many stories below us.

"No. The boom was already here when I found the place. It saved me the trouble of rigging a zip line." He obviously prepared a lot more than I did. Making me wonder how much of my survival I owed to dumb luck.

"What if we get to the ground and they're already there?" Because, hey, why not start panicking now?

"I'd worry more about the ones the fire didn't stop that are now on the roof."

I glanced overhead in time to see a mutant leaping over the edge!

## CHAPTER 14

"Incoming!" I screamed as the mutant with a few extra limp legs and a green-and-gray-hued carapace, plummeted in our direction, eyes bright with insanity.

"I see it." What did Xavion do with the warning? Rocked the fucking scaffold.

I screamed as I held on. "You crazy fucking bastard!"

"Stay out of the way," yelled as Xavion pulled his sword and swung.

Just in time. He knocked the mutant away. I didn't look but assumed gravity applied and pulled it to the ground where it couldn't hurt us.

One down.

I glanced up and didn't need him to say, "Stay sharp, Lia. We've got more incoming company."

No shit. I saw them overhead. Heads peeking over the edge, looking human until they leaned too far and showed their mandibled, misshaped mouths.

Metal screamed as Xavion screwed with the mechanism. The scaffold jerked as we began to plummet a little bit faster.

We were doing great until we jolted to a stop. Lopsided, I might add. The whole contraption tilted, and I held on even tighter.

Xavion braced and leaned against the incline, glaring upward. "We need to get off."

"We're only halfway to the ground."

"I know. But they're not giving us a choice. They've figured out to screw with the ropes."

They as in the mutants. Why were they being so persistent?

A glance upward showed one grabbing hold of the cables to shimmy down.

Oh fuck.

I didn't even think. I pulled my gun and aimed. Hit my target, which yelped and fell off, glancing off the railing and sending us rocking.

I almost fell out.

Xavion exclaimed, "Mind not shooting at the only thing holding us up?"

"I couldn't exactly let it climb in with us," I remarked. Miffed he'd not congratulated me. Embarrassed that dumb luck had saved the cable. I'd not even thought of it when I fired.

"We're sitting humans here," he muttered. A chilling change on an old expression.

Quack.

An ululation of excitement drew my gaze upward in time to see a mutant throw itself over the edge. It leaped too far and missed us.

"They're not going to stop," I muttered, glancing at the next one preparing to leap. So many of them. What the hell?

"We need to get off this thing." Xavion used the hilt of his sword to rap the window. Harder. It did nothing.

"We don't have time for this," I grumbled. Gun already out, I fired. The window splintered, and a sweep of his sword cleared the many jagged shards.

He leapt in first and offered his hand. I didn't need it but appreciated it as I clambered in after him. Just in time.

A body plummeted from above and hit our scaffold hard enough it snapped. It swung like a broken pendulum.

Gulp. Just a few more seconds...

A flash of light caught my attention.

Xavion had lit the dusty couch on fire. "Quick. We need to get downstairs before them." He held my hand and pulled me out of the apartment. We raced down the hall and into the stairwell. My heart pounded. I heard skittering and hooting as the monsters above us noticed and changed direction.

"They're coming," I huffed.

Xavion had more tricks. The landing held a bottle I'd never noticed before tucked under the first step. He pulled it and squirted, leaving a big puddle at the end that he dropped his lit Zippo into.

Whoosh.

I had an irrational craving for marshmallows before giving myself a shake. He'd bought a minute at most, possibly only seconds.

Our footsteps boomed as we raced, the debris in the landings now making more sense. Xavion had planted them there, and given the sudden flare of light and heat as one of them ignited, I had a feeling he might have planted some flammable items too.

"We need to get out of here," he confirmed, which

led to a final burst of speed. We took the final two landings in leaps and bounds. We burst onto the street but only ran a few paces before stopping and whirling.

The apartment building was on fire. The apartment he'd lit had its windows glowing, and inside the front doors, the lobby was getting rosy cozy.

I pretended to not hear the screams as monsters burned alive.

"We did it."

Survived to see another day.

But lost our home.

Where would we go?

## CHAPTER 15

"W<sub>e</sub> need to get out of the city, at least until things calm down," Xavion declared.

"No shit." Seeing that many mutants in one place, cooperating in an effort to kill us? "Where are you thinking?"

"I have a farm."

"Wait, what? You're a farmer?" He was too sexy. I remembered Old McDonald. He wore coveralls, ate a piece of hay, and had chubby cheeks and twinkling eyes under his straw hat.

"Not really. I don't raise many animals or anything, but I have a small garden."

He almost sounded embarrassed as we walked away from the fire, alert because humans weren't supposed to roam at night.

"You grow stuff."

"Yeah. But mostly, I hunt and use that to get people to help me. That and let them keep some too."

"Why are you in the city if you can live off your farm?" The very idea made me wonder.

"I told you, I hunt."

He might, but if I had the choice to live in relative safety, with fresh food? Hello, country living. I'd learn to put my hair in pigtails, cut my jeans into daisy dukes, and make my own pickles.

"How will we get there?" I asked.

"I have a bike stashed in that alley." He pointed.

Dumb me, I thought he meant a motorcycle.

When I saw it, my dumb reply was, "It's a bike."

"Yeah."

"With no motor."

"Doesn't need gas."

A good point. Who knew gas could go bad? By the time I figured it out, I was stuck in the city.

"I only see one," I pointed out. A nice bike, matte black, with a rack and a basket that I wouldn't make fun of. At least it didn't have a bell. Always hated those stupid things. Listening to a podcast while walking to the subway and some psycho in spandex would go whipping by on the sidewalk ringing it nonstop.

"We can double up until we find you a ride of your own," he said,

Which meant, while he stood and pedaled, I sat on the set, legs splayed, holding on to his ass.

The ride ended outside a sporting goods store not too badly damaged. With me keeping watch, he found one he said would be great for off-roading. I sweated bullets, not daring to blink at the dark while he inflated the flat tires.

Only as I sat on it did I admit, "I never learned to ride a bike as a kid."

"It's easy."

Said the man who didn't keep falling over.

"I've got an idea," he said when I sniffled on the floor because my body hurt after the third fall.

The training wheels on my bike were humiliating. Good thing no one was around to see. I took a spin on them in the store. They were really freaking noisy.

Xavion grimaced. "That won't do."

"I'm sorry. This is my fault. My mom said bikes were dangerous. I wasn't even allowed on the swings at the park." Having read all the books I could find, I'd had time to examine my upbringing and admit my mom never let me experience enough. Never had I regretted it more than in this moment. Because of me, we couldn't make a getaway.

"I'll figure something out." It took only fifteen minutes before his bike gained a third wheel with a seat and handlebars. A tag-along or so the box claimed. Used by children so they could ride with their parent. Or, in this case, for a woman who'd grown up in a concrete jungle.

With our three-wheeled machine, we made good time. It was liberating to ride in the open at night. I'd never been so bold. Now tell my instincts to stop screaming, *Hide. Hide. Hide.*

If I'd been hiding, I would have never met Xavion. Never realized I could still live.

We rode that entire night and only barely stopped. We couldn't ride straight out of the city because some of the roads were blocked. Intentionally, which chilled me.

The fatigue began setting in around three a.m. according to my watch. And then I heard it. An ululating shriek to our left.

"We've been spotted!" were his grim words as he pedaled harder.

For the last few hours until dawn, that shrieking

followed us, growing fainter as we left the crowded spaces of the city for the more spread-out suburbia.

And farther still.

Only when the sun fully bathed the land did we stop for a rest. I collapsed on a front lawn grown long and lush. Basked in the rays. With him lying beside me, I fell asleep. And he must have, too, because, next thing we knew, a rude voice woke us.

"What have we here, boys?" said a guy missing most of his front teeth blocking my sunlight.

"Dinner and dessert."

**CHAPTER 16**

A PITY MORE OF HUMANITY WASN'T LIKE Xavion. Yes, he'd seduced me upon meeting, but he asked and ensured he got consent. Wanted my willingness.

The thugs who woke us from our nap? The kind of assholes who thought it was okay to reach for a woman to do unspeakable things.

Wrong move.

Xavion wasn't the type to sit calmly by.

Sure, the one with the big goofy ears held a knife on my boyfriend, but Xavion looked pissed more than anything.

So I wasn't surprised when he reacted, the movement sharp and sudden, Big Ears' head snapping back before Toothless even managed to finish grabbing me.

As Big Ears started to scream and Toothless gaped even wider, Xavion took them out.

One with a knife to the heart, the other a bullet between his surprised eyes.

Xavion was cold as ice when he said, "Run or you die too."

Who did he speak to?

The third thug, holding a piece of wood with jagged nails on the porch behind us, gaped then ran.

I blinked and said, "That was really fucking hot."

Our lips met, and we couldn't help ourselves. Stripping in the open was dumb—we'd just been attacked—but his hand down my pants and mine around his dick meant mutual masturbation to culmination.

Yes. I came. Yes. We lived.

We continued our trip but at a more leisurely pace, moving well past suburbia to where the land held untamed spaces. Where the air smelled of possibility. Where birds still flew in the sky.

The fields had been mowed in some areas. Others held tall corn stalks growing wild and sporadically.

Fucking corn, though. I wouldn't starve.

I could have cried. Maybe the world hadn't truly ended. Maybe we could ride far enough we'd find civilization again or at least an easier way of life.

Foolish and yet I couldn't help but wonder.

It was midafternoon when we rode up a driveway to a cute little house. Made of gray river stone with a porch and a tree heavy with apples.

Apples!

I almost tipped us both in my haste to get off the bike and run for the fruit.

Xavion didn't share my enthusiasm but rather glanced around suspiciously.

"What's wrong?" I asked, mouth full of crunchy, mushy sweetness.

"The fruit. No one's picked it."

Some littered the ground, going bad. What a waste. I took another bite. "You have someone apple picking for you?"

"Yes, in exchange, they keep half."

I slowed my enthusiastic eating. "You think something happened."

The gun emerged. "Stay close."

He prowled through his house—a place of comfort strewn with big furniture and a room dedicated entirely to books. More than I could read in a lifetime—a challenge I looked forward to beating.

Another bedroom had stacks of clothes and boxes of shoes. Not just for men. Women and what seemed like children's wear too. He'd been hoarding and not stupid shit like jewelry. I'd met some people who thought surrounding themselves in the past's trappings made them wealthy. I saw riches differently these days.

Could it clothe me? Feed me? Defend me? Love me...

As we went through the house, we saw no signs of anyone having entered. All his traps remained intact, yet that pinched expression didn't leave his face.

"I need to go out for a bit. Lock the door after I leave."

I sounded way too whiny and codependent when I said, "Where are you going?"

"To check on my neighbor."

"The one who didn't pick the apples?"

"Yeah. He and his wife aren't getting any younger."

How could I refuse?

I did demand a kiss and a promise. "Come back to me."

"Depends...What's in it for me?" he teased.

"Epic blow job." I'd give him two if it brought

him back safe.

"Well hell, I would have settled for a kiss." He got one. Two. Three.

He peeled me from him. "I gotta go."

"Maybe I should go with you."

He shook his head. "It'll be faster if I go alone. Plus I need to warn Benoit about you. He can be trigger-happy with strangers."

With that final warning, he left, and I paced. So much for my belief the country was safer.

It took forever—twenty-seven minutes according to my clock, which I wound religiously every week—before he returned.

I sat behind the bolted front door, shotgun in my lap.

He rapped. "Lia, it's me."

I flung open the door and grabbed Xavion in a hug. I'd known him long enough to realize I didn't want to lose him.

He held me tight and whispered, "It's okay."

"Is it? How's your neighbor?"

"Dead."

I leaned back enough to see his face. "What killed him?"

A bleak expression tugged his features. "A bullet to his head. His wife wasn't feeling good last time I saw them. Some kind of chest infection. Guess it got worse. I saw a handmade cross over a freshly dug spot in his front yard. I don't think he took it well."

I could only hug him tighter. I understood the loneliness. Worse than anything I could imagine, but at the same time, I'd mostly been alone before the apocalypse. How much worse would it be to lose someone, to be thrust into solitude after having had the companionship of someone you loved?

What would I do if I lost Xavion?

I didn't need to say anything. He understood. Probably felt the same way I did.

Desperate. And needy. What if this was our last moment? Shouldn't we enjoy it?

With clumsy fingers, I attacked his clothes. I wanted him naked so I could reassure myself he'd returned unharmed. I needed to feel his flesh. In moments, we were naked, and I was being carried to our bed.

The sheets still held the crisp scent of being dried outdoors. But it was the scent of him, the musk, the heat that I craved. I tugged him down to me so that his heavy body covered mine.

We kissed, our tongues meshing with a familiarity that always thrilled. The head of his hard cock nudged the petals of my sex.

I was tempted to let him in, to have him fill me with his cock. But I had made a promise.

I broke off the kiss to give him an order, "Lie on your back."

"You want to ride?" He grinned as he rolled over.

"Maybe, but first, I think I owe you something for coming back in one piece."

"You don't have to...Ah." He gasped as I ignored him and grabbed his jutting dick.

I loved looking at it. Long. Thick. Slightly curved. Just right to bring me pleasure.

Was it any wonder I loved pleasing him?

One hand gripped him tight, and my other cupped his sac, kneading it. His cock pulsed in my hand.

I leaned forward and took it into my mouth, tasting the saltiness of his excitement. I gave him a little suck.

He sighed.

I almost smiled, but cock sucking was serious business. I bathed his cock with my tongue, swirling it around, exploring every inch before I took him into my mouth. I loved sucking him. Watching him trying to act as if he had control.

He didn't.

His hands fisted the sheets. His hips twitched. His dick pulsed in my mouth.

When I started a fast bob, his head arched and his neck went taut. The balls I kneaded and fondled drew tight.

He groaned. "I'm going to come if you don't stop."

"Good."

"Not good," he growled. "I want to be inside you."

He flipped me onto my back, and my legs parted that he might thrust into me. He pumped me with his big dick. Drove into me over and over until I gasped and knew my nails must be leaving marks in his shoulder.

I was going to come.

I was so close...

And that bastard slipped out.

But I forgave him when he replaced his cock with his tongue. He licked between my nether lips, teasing me before he concentrated on my clit. He flicked it with his tongue and sucked it, driving me wild.

Bringing me to the brink.

Until I came.

I shuddered and climaxed, but he wasn't done.

He slid into me and began thrusting. Over and over until I trembled and squeezed.

I came with a loud scream. And still he kept pounding, drawing out my orgasm, until somewhere around the third wave, he came too.

And said the thing I'd been thinking but was too scared to speak aloud.

"I love you."

**CHAPTER 17**

ONCE XAVION SAID IT, I WAS FREED TO SAY IT too. And I did, over and over.

If I thought I was happy before, this was paradise in comparison.

Me and my man, with our own little place. Working the land. Him mostly. I still had a killer thumb. Instead of growing things, I learned how to pickle and jar fruit. I just hoped I did it right so we had some all winter.

We settled into a routine, one that still had us locked inside at night but cozy in our bed.

So why was I determined to ruin it? Tracing circles on his chest, about a week after our arrival, I blurted out, "Have you given up on eliminating the mutants?"

"Maybe I found something better to dedicate my life to."

That reply got him the best sex of his life. Still, I couldn't help but think about it later.

He'd been doing something good. That might make a difference. Especially now that I knew the mutants might be working together.

I ended up asking him, "What are the chances the mutants come after us?"

He rolled his shoulders. "Honestly? No fucking clue. I just know if they dare come out here, then we'll deal with them. But I doubt we'll have many to worry about. As the monsters get older, they'll start dying off. Winter is especially harsh on them."

I tried to feel his confidence and yet couldn't help a certain disquiet wondering if we were in the eye of the storm.

My trepidation gave away to excitement when, two weeks after our arrival, he said, "Get yourself dolled up. We're going to market."

I might have stopped breathing. I know my eyeballs dried out as I forgot to blink. I managed a zombie-like, "Whaaaa?"

"Market. The full moon is almost here, which is the designated time for those who want to meet at the country fairgrounds to swap stuff."

It sank in. "We're going shopping!" Be still, my screaming girly heart. Until it occurred to me, "We don't have a car to bring stuff home."

"Or anything to pull a carriage, meaning we can only bring and trade what we can carry ourselves."

"Carry?" There went my dream of coming home laden with packages.

"With the two of us, we'll be able to get a whole bunch of stuff. Good thing you learned to ride that bike."

He'd insisted on teaching me how to not only ride on two wheels by myself but then proceeded to teach me how to handle small jumps while going at fast speed—in case we needed to escape.

Turned out my fear of having to carry stuff, or balance it on my handlebars, was unfounded. My bike—a bright purple with streamers—acquired a trailer on the back, the kind used before by yuppie mommies and daddies to drag their kids around.

Since we'd pickled and jarred enough already for our own use, we loaded the trailers with the leftover apples. Too many for the two of us to consume. Xavion also had stuff he brought out of the garage, cartons of smokes, a few bottles of booze, one of tequila that I bargained my virtue right then and there for.

"You get the stuff that can't be made from the city," I remarked as we headed off.

"Yup. Foraging is why I can avoid becoming a full-time farmer."

"But you look sexy in jeans and cowboy boots." When he took that shirt off and sweated in the fall afternoon sun, I usually showed him how much.

He grinned at me. "And you were made for plaid."

Once upon a time, I would have gone naked before wearing any. Now? I enjoyed my plaid jammies that kept me warm on chilly autumn nights.

"How far is this place?"

"Only a few miles."

Miles that had traffic. Of sorts.

A man with an honest-to-goodness wagon being pulled by some big cow-looking beasts. Only they lacked the milk titty underneath. A few people cantered by on horses.

I gaped like a country bumpkin. Tears filled my eyes, too, enough I had to stop, which drew Xavion close to ask, "What's wrong?"

"People." It was the only word I managed to sob. Not just a couple but an actual community's worth. It gave me hope that maybe, just maybe, humans could rebuild. Start over.

As things got busy, we got off our bikes and pulled them, the weight of the apples not so easy over the trampled grass of the field. Some folks, like us, wandered with little carts or bulging packs. Others, like the guy with the wagon, parked and waited for potential traders to come to him.

We were one of them, trading all the apples in my cart for eggs, cured ham, and a promise from a fellow, name of Roland, who would deliver two chickens the following week.

I was ridiculously excited.

As the swapping happened, elation and the hum of animated conversation filled the air. I didn't see the avarice and violence from the city. Nor the desperation.

Hope shone in these faces. Life flourished. I saw more than a few pregnant bellies and babies. Children darted around all over, laughing with the joy of youth.

They'd yet to understand everything they'd lost. And frankly, as they grew older, they'd never know any different.

This was the new normal.

We were in this together.

And together, we were horrified when a child

came screaming at the top of his lungs, "Monster took Cassidy!"

## CHAPTER 18

IMMEDIATELY, XAVION LEFT ME WITH OUR STUFF and ran to the group forming around the boy. As they questioned him, the hum and mood of the crowd changed. People began packing up and moving away rapidly.

But not everyone.

Xavion stood with a group of fierce-looking people and one sobbing woman being held by a man.

Xavion's gaze met mine, and he excused himself to get close enough to mutter, "You need to stay here."

"Seriously? I can help."

"I know you can, but if you stay, you can help guard those left, and our stuff." I glanced at our loot.

A tragedy didn't mean everyone turned into a saint. The temptation to steal might be too strong.

"Come back safe. Please." I kissed him, and while I wanted to beg him to say, I wouldn't. Because he'd do this no matter what. The chances of the child being found alive were slim, but the armed group, led by Xavion, weren't about to let the monster keep her.

As the sun crept farther across the sky, I began to worry for my own safety. It took us over an hour getting here. I didn't look forward to making the same trek at night.

With the sun beginning to dip, and my panic getting close to full blown, especially as every one but the parents of the missing girl took off, the search party returned, shoulders down. And a few less than what had left.

No little person with them. The mother who'd lost her child playing tag in the field sobbed.

Xavion said nothing as he neared me. His haunted face, the blood on his clothes, said it all.

"Bad?" I asked.

"The only good news is we killed them all so they won't be taking any more children."

As we rode hard for our house, our damned carriages feeling more like a weight than treasure, I couldn't help but notice how intent Xavion was. He didn't speak, only rode hard, slightly behind me, guarding my flank.

Him worrying worried me and pushed me past my usual limits of endurance. We didn't make it to the house before nightfall, and the dark was full of spooky noises. I was soaked in an acrid sweat by the time we arrived. But that didn't stop me from helping him unload and put our shit away.

Only then did we lock ourselves inside. The cistern he'd rigged on the roof meant I could run him a bath. I tossed some fragrant herbs I'd swapped for in the water and stripped Xavion.

I washed his tense body until the words finally spilled from him. "There were fifteen of them."

The number staggered.

"And that little girl wasn't the only one," he added softly. "The others were taken on their way in by the looks of it. They didn't even need that little girl. They had enough food. She was taken to taunt us."

The claim made me pause for a second. "What makes you say that?"

"Because they killed the child but didn't eat her. They left her in a clearing for us to find as bait."

"Wait, they set a trap for you?"

"An ambush, only it failed and only because we caught on. Had Franklin not realized we were being herded, we might have all died.

"Once we killed them all, we stumbled across their camp. They'd taken over a house by a river. Were sleeping in the barn. They had thrown the bodies they were done with in the old pig sty."

I put my hand over my mouth. "And no one knew they were there?"

He shook his head.

"I thought they didn't leave the city much."

His lips pursed. "Not usually. Why does any animal leave its territory?"

Food.

And we all knew what the mutants liked to eat.

"What does this mean?"

He sighed and leaned his head back, eyes closed. "It means tomorrow we need to track down the stragglers from the ambush and start sweeping for others."

Knowing he would leave made our lovemaking extra special that night. Slow. We remained eyes locked the entire time. Connected on a level that I'd never imagined and didn't want to lose.

"I love you," his last words to me as he set off to rid the world of monsters.

He returned. Dirty, bloody again, but with good

news. They'd found the hiding spot of some mutants, an even dozen this time. and cleaned them out.

Given what they found, the next day, they planned to sweep in a different direction lest a nest of mutants fester still nearby.

I armed myself. "I'm going with you."

He shook his head. "We can't both go. The last of the crops have to be harvested. The coop built before the chickens arrive."

I arched a brow. "And you think I'm qualified to do that?"

A rueful grin tugged his lips. "Is it sexist to want you here where it's safe?"

Yes, but also sweet, and loving, too, which was why I retorted, "I'm a better hunter than farmer."

He dragged me close. "I can't lose you."

My voice choked as I said, "You think I don't feel the same way?"

I knew I'd won when he sighed. "Fine. But you stay close to me." Something he reiterated as we entered a dense forest just as the clouds rolled in, darkening the land.

In the city, I only went out on sunny days. Out here? I had nowhere to lock myself in. But I'd asked for this. Demanded to be a part. I couldn't turn coward now.

Part of our group, Leroy with the golden beard and bald head, said, "I've got a bad feeling about this."

We all did.

Turned out, we should have yellow-bellied and run.

## CHAPTER 19

THERE WAS NO WARNING, JUST MUTANTS suddenly dropping from trees. So many of them, and taking us by surprise. Mutants were supposed to hide in darkness during the day.

Someone forgot to give these ugly fuckers the memo.

I fired wildly before losing my gun, knocked aside by an arm that ended in a spidery tip. Around me, I heard more shooting, lots of screaming, and I could taste the fear in the air.

I'd pulled my knife and stabbed anything that got near, too panicked to make sure it wasn't an ally.

"Cecilia!" I heard Xavion yell my name, but turning to look for him proved a mistake.

The blow to my head dropped me, and when I

woke, I thought I must still be having a nightmare because I'd have never put myself in the dank dark place that chilled me to the bone.

I pushed myself to a sitting position, my head aching, my senses spinning. Something lay across my legs pinning them, and I reached to push. My fingers met flesh. Dead flesh.

My stomach emptied, so hard I almost popped my eyeballs. Great, just fucking great.

I struggled to my feet and swayed. Where was I?

Pit of Hell came to mind. The rancid smell made me think of rotting meat. The whispery and scratchy sense of movement around didn't reassure.

The sudden light in the darkness had me blinking to adjust. I wish I'd remained blind.

I'd not been far off the mark. I was in Hell.

Mutant Hell. Surrounded by them, their human eyes, at odds with the alien features.

The light, a simple solar-based lantern, sat on the base of a pile of bones. Human judging by the skulls. Atop it perched a monster. Its exoskeleton a deep red with dark streaks. No hair on its head, its lips black and thick.

"She wakessss." The voice didn't sound right. Probably on account the mandibles gave the mutant an accent.

"What do you want?" I swear, if he said eat me alive, I'd probably piss myself. Would they consider that flavor?

"Want the hunter."

"The what?"

"The hunter. The one who kills us. He and the others musssst die." A sentence ended on a sibilant hiss that his entourage repeated.

They wanted Xavion. Holy shit. He must have been doing more damage than even he realized. I took a closer look around me, at the monsters staring upon me with hunger. Now that I paid attention, I could see the age in many of them. The damage.

But it took my mind a moment to comprehend the bulging belly on an obvious female with pendulous teats, the flesh of her abdomen roiling as if alive, the skin pushing and pulsing.

"Dear Lord, what's wrong with her."

"She carries my children." Hissed with glee.

Gag. This was wrong. So fucking wrong. Surely the mutants couldn't procreate? Even Xavion assumed they couldn't. How could we have been so wrong?

"That doesn't look healthy," I pointed out at the skin stretched hard enough I expected it to split.

"One for the many." The monster king's chuckle grated like nails on glass.

"That's harsh."

"Harsh is your hunter. Killer."

"Because you're sick."

"Not sick. The future." The word hung in the air.

The future was a spider baby, sporting too many legs, a bobbly head, and a drooling grin that suddenly scrambled up the pile of bones to visit its daddy long legs.

Maybe a braver person wouldn't have fainted.

That person wasn't me.

## CHAPTER 20

I'd been kidnapped midday, and when I next woke, I had no idea how many hours had passed. What I could be certain of was Xavion would be an idiot to try and save me.

The mutant monster king had an army, and even if these were bottom of the barrel, they had the numbers to overwhelm.

The realization I'd die should have sent me into hysterics. After all, didn't I deserve a good cry? This sucked. I'd finally found happiness, and now I'd end up as a mutant dinner.

Would I just give in to my fate?

I remained in the same place as before, I could tell by the vomit. The mutants hovered on the outer edges, just out of the light that kept glowing.

The monster king had left his throne, but spider baby remained perched on it, hanging with its spindly limbs. Terrifying with its curly mop of hair and very alien face.

When it hissed, its mandibles spread like flower petals and I saw the layers of teeth inside.

No surprise, I'd lost all my weapons. Knife, gun, other knife. I had nothing to defend myself—or to end my life in a way that didn't involve teeth or claws.

Oddly, in the face of hopelessness, I found courage and determination. There had to be a way. As I stirred in my nest of filth, I realized it was comprised of remnants. Clothing scraps, left on the ground, stiff with dried blood and other fluids.

What excited me? Seeing a pack of cigarettes partially expelled from a plaid shirt pocket. Where there were smokes, there was usually—

A lighter. I didn't waste time and ignited the piece of cloth closest to me.

It didn't go unnoticed.

"Fire!" Apparently not just the monster king could speak. Someone noticed the flame I lit. Before they could swarm, I lit some more stuff, not all of it catching as well as I'd like, but as the little flames began to flicker, and the light increased, I noticed something interesting.

The mutants recoiled.

And then they began to leave.

Animal Kingdom 101. Fire equals run.

As the flames grew brighter, I realized we were in a movie theatre, the concession area to be exact. No windows inside, and the whole thing surrounded by doors to go inside theatres. And if I knew one thing, all theatres had a door to the outside in case of a fire.

Given it would be dark, and dangerous, I sought out a weapon. I grabbed a leg bone and tried to ignore the fact it appeared gnawed on. I wrapped the plaid shirt that had the smokes around it. I lit it like a torch from my still sizzling first fire. It went suddenly from the cloth I'd lit to the carpet. The same carpet I stood on.

Time to leave. I aimed for theatre number eight. The door for it opened easily, and with my fiery wand waving ahead, I entered.

The rows of seats marched down to the floor in front of the stage. Most theatres still placed the screen upon one.

I saw no one, but I didn't trust the shadows. As I walked, my skin prickled, convinced of the eyes watching. The way I tensed, surely they ganged up behind me, preparing to pounce.

The belief led to me whirling and waving my torch. Nothing. Just in case...I lit the carpet behind me on fire.

I just hoped I'd not fucked myself if I had to go back out that way. I ran down the rest of the steps and had almost made it to the bottom when a door to the outside opened and I was confronted by none of than the hissing baby mama.

She didn't look human at all. Her eyes black and multifaceted, her mandibles rouged and lined in sharp jagged points.

"I don't suppose you'll step aside." I kept moving, waving my torch in front of me.

Despite the roiling belly in front of her, she led with clawed fingers and hissed as she dove at me.

I dodged and swung my torch, drawing a squeal. But she didn't heed my warning.

I'd be honest, monster or not, I didn't want to kill baby mama, so when she came at me again, swinging and spitting, I waved my torch, only to try and get her away from me.

Only she danced out of reach, and too late I realized she played the part of distraction.

Arms—legs, something!—wrapped around me

from behind. I screamed as my limbs were pinned and felt the heat of my own torch against my leg. I couldn't swing it, only drop it.

The carpet caught fire as if waiting for this moment. Baby mama squealed and scurried, and my captor might have carried me along, only I went into a frenzy of motion. Legs kicking. Head slamming back. I got the mutant to let go, and I hit the floor, close enough to flames that I might not have any eyebrows left.

I ran for the exit, with only a glowing X left to mark it. The push bar gave easily, and I spilled outside, gulping the fresh air. Wanting to sob in relief.

I'd done it. Escaped.

Almost. I should get away from the building. Quickly.

I had no idea where I was. So I just started running, following the pavement of the parking lot, figuring it would spill onto a road eventually. I didn't get far.

Something landed in front of me, with a bend of springy legs. Judging by his snarl, the monster king wasn't happy with me.

"Take her!" he bellowed.

Boing. Boing. It began to rain Arachans, the

name that began trending on social media before it went dark forever.

Six of them surrounded me. Not weak like those I'd seen before. They had all their parts and appeared strong.

I wouldn't be able to outrun them. As to fighting? Not successfully without a weapon.

I eyed the door behind me. Perhaps the flames would be preferable.

It was then I heard the most unexpected, and beautiful, thing.

"Let her go or I put a bullet in her head."

Xavion had come for me.

## CHAPTER 21

THE BELLY EMERGED BEFORE XAVION DID. HE held the pregnant Arachvid mommy-to-be by the hair.

She hissed and twisted. But he'd wrapped her hands behind her and shoved her ahead, while keeping out his gun.

"Do anything stupid and she dies."

If the monster king cared for her, this could work.

But monsters didn't have feelings. "Kill her. I'll find another mate."

Baby momma didn't look happy at the answer. And ran for the king, hissing. He batted her aside without any regard.

I couldn't tell if she lived or not, given how quickly scurrying bodies carried her away.

Didn't care. I focused on the important.

Xavion had come for me. Romantic and stupid and I loved him for it even as I feared for him.

One man against an army of mutants. It didn't look good, but I wouldn't give up. He'd defied odds to save me. Now I'd have to do my best to save us both.

Could I count on dawn to save the day?

Inside the building, I'd been unable to tell time. Outside, all I knew was dawn didn't hint at all yet in the sky. Night gripped the land, which meant the mutants spilled from the burning movie theatre in numbers that didn't bode well for me or my man.

Only he'd not come alone.

"Now!" he yelled.

I wondered at his plan when I was blinded by the light. Literally. The brightness of it must have held some UV strength because I heard screeching, and even better some of the mutants retreated, some back into the burning theater, others to the shadows past it.

The monster king was one of only a dozen that didn't flinch in the light—the most human seeming of the bunch, who were also armed with big knives and even a gun.

"Get him. Kill the hunter," hissed the monster king. Points for him recognizing the threat posed by my man. But apparently, a misogynist in life remained one as a mutant. The monster king had forgotten about me.

I didn't need anything fancy. I didn't know where the twisted hunk of metal came from, didn't care other than the fact it made a most excellent club.

I swung and connected, knocking the spider king but not taking him out. He whirled on me and spat. Like literally, a gob of goo that I barely avoided.

It hit the ground, and I swear I heard it sizzle. Even if that was my imagination, nothing good would come of being slimed. I faced off against the monster, weapon in hand as he advanced, flexing his claws.

"Behind you!" Xavion yelled.

I whirled in time to block a recovered baby mama as she sprang at me. Didn't she know all that jostling was probably bad for the fetuses?

We struggled, and I worried about the monster king, only to hear Xavion nearby saying, "Pick on someone your own size, ugly."

Would it be offensive if I told the pregnant one to go away and find someone her size as well?

She screamed as she thrashed with me. Her mandibles clacked, and I flinched. The poor thing. She might have been normal and pretty once upon a time. She'd not asked to be like this.

I also couldn't let her live to be a threat. Not her or the monsters she carried. But I wasn't cruel about it.

A jugular slash with the piece of glass I'd snared was all it took. I did what I had to and didn't watch.

I whirled to see Xavion facing off against the monster king, sword in hand. The blade swung and the monster king parried the blows off wrist shields comprised of thick layers of carapace. The monster had some naturally made armor covering his chest as well too. A species adapting.

How terrifying.

Especially recalling the king's words. Surely a monstrous perversion of humanity wasn't the future.

The sword got knocked out of Xavion's grip, leaving him facing off, hands empty, against the king, who appeared more expansive than before.

The king raised an arm that instead of ending in a hand, was more like a scythe. He began to slice the air with it, about to gut my lover.

Xavion pulled a gun and shot it point-blank. In the head.

He then ducked to avoid the last movement of the dying king.

The body hit the ground, and a stillness suddenly filled the air. The mutants fighting those who'd accompanied Xavion paused. I saw the moment they registered the death. They scattered and ran, some inside, others for the town outskirts, where the theater was situated.

I half expected him to chase after. The mutants posed a danger, but he opened his arms and dragged me close.

The hug of all hugs. A grossly sweaty one. But I didn't care. We both lived.

I kissed him. "I can't believe you came for me."

"Can't be Adam without my Eve," he said, cupping my ass.

"I love you."

"Love you more. And I'll show you how much once we get out of here." We headed off with the group who'd joined him, the man with the wagon having brought the solar generator and the bank of lights. While a few of them got a ride in the wheeled cart, others set off on horseback to hunt down the stragglers.

I sat behind Xavion, holding on for dear life as he

trotted away from the shooting flames in the movie theatre.

"You came prepared," I said, as my ass discovered it wasn't into horseback riding.

"I wasn't losing you." Said so seriously.

I could only lean my cheek on his back and be happy to know I was loved.

"Where are we going?" I asked.

"Home."

We arrived just as dawn crested.

Two returning survivors. Lovers.

Walking into the sunset, having escaped death.

He just had to ruin the moment by saying, "Want to repopulate the world?"

Was he nuts? Did he know the havoc pregnancy would wreak on my body? My poor vajajay would never be the same, not to mention the possibilities of complications.

Selfish me filled my head first.

New me, the one who recognized each day as precious, smiled.

"They say practice makes perfect."

We practiced the moment we got home. Right in our sunny front yard. His only regret? The sunburn on his bare ass, which I delighted in slapping.

## EPILOGUE

THAT WASN'T THE FIRST NEST WE ERADICATED. Or the last time we were in danger. We could have chosen to barricade ourselves in our happy little home and pretended the ugly didn't exist, but I couldn't stop thinking of that little girl. Stolen from under her parents' noses.

What if that happened to our child? The one growing inside me.

What if a mutant ate the one doctor we had? Sure, in his old life, Dr. Weiner dealt with farm animals, but a baby was a baby. Right?

It meant we couldn't be complacent. Not if our child was to be safe. As we secured the area around us, we also put up signs, inviting others to join us, which caused controversy. It might invite the wrong sort. But then again, anyone who managed to survive deserved a chance. Not everyone turned to violence because they wanted to.

We would remind people what it meant to be civil. To support one another.

To not hide in shadows.

And find love like I had.

Hard to believe that humanity had found a new beginning in me. Hope I didn't kill it like our garden.

Ps. I made edible pickles.

Pss. We don't talk about the failed attempt at jam.

Psss. In case you wondered, we had a girl and named her Laura after his mom.

And we lived happily ever after in our rebooted world.

**LOOKING FOR MORE APOCALYPSE ROMANCE?**
SEE EVELANGLAIS.COM